See Beneath Your Perfect

A See Beneath Novel

Eunice Nascimento

ISBN-13: 9781838477134

Cover design by: Olinart

To you, Mum. You loved and lost. Then you found the courage to love again. Thank you for being my mum.

Prologue

Four Years In The Past.

Before that moment, when the dirt blanketed Catarina's casket like a macabre cocoon protecting its baby, it hadn't been real. Mo had pretended she was still somewhere in the world, visiting friends like she frequently did. Because that was Catarina—always alive, always laughing, always out with friends. That's how he'd rationalised the emptiness on the other side of the bed, the vacant chair at the breakfast table, his solo morning commute and her absence at dinner. She'd gone away for a few days. Now, he could no longer pretend. The nightmare that started two weeks ago on what was supposed to be the happiest day of their lives had to be faced.

Someone patted his shoulder. Mo understood—he'd been to enough funerals to know it was time for friends and family to say goodbye. But he couldn't bring himself to look away from Catarina and the dirt piling high. How was he supposed to say goodbye? Father Thomas' words of condolence didn't help. Nothing did. Nothing made the ache go away.

He'd been angry before—angry with Catarina, angry with himself. He'd cried and begged God, hoping it was all a dream and Catarina would wake up. But that didn't happen, and now he was only numb.

Mo clenched his fists. Nothing made sense. His legs gave way, felling him to the newly disturbed earth. Memories of Catarina rushed into his mind.

They were seventeen, and he told her he loved her for the first time as they hid in the school gym to get away from their friends. Heart pounding, he'd looked into her brown-black eyes and confessed his strong feelings, terrified that she'd reject him.

At twenty-four, on their university grounds, she gave him the biggest surprise of his life by proposing to him on results day. That was the first time he'd cried since he was a child—their happiness as fresh in his mind on this terrible day as it was on that wonderful one.

They were twenty-six on their wedding day, a vast affair organised by their parents even though they'd wanted a small ceremony so they could save up to buy a house. "I'll love you forever. You're the love of my life," Mo said to Catarina before they walked down the aisle and the mayhem of the guests enveloped them.

He'd repeated those words when Catarina told him she was keeping the baby they'd conceived three years after their marriage, even though he'd wanted her to finish her specialisation before they had children.

There would be no more memories to add to these. Their happy life together cut short during labour when doctors tore Catarina away from him and into the operating room. A rare excessive bleeding complication, they had said. They saved the baby, but it had been too late for Catarina.

Mo stroked the mound of dirt from his prone position staring hard at Catarina's picture propped against the flowers in front of his face. He spoke the only words his heart would allow, "I promise to love you forever. You will be the only woman in my life."

"We need to go. The cemetery is closing."

Mo wasn't sure who said those words. Hands lifted him, and he shuffled his feet as his brothers Noah and Eli and friends Brad and Tae Joon walked beside him. The sun, which had previously been a blazing orb, was now a tiny pink glow on the horizon.

Chapter 1

"The next station is Hackney Central."

Mo stood right in the middle of the door, where it would open first. He checked his watch, willing the hands to crawl but, they flew whenever he was late. Unbidden, his fingers tapped on the satchel flung across his body. As soon as the doors began to inch open, he squeezed out, rushing through the passengers milling about the station. He sprinted through the cemetery to the beautiful tombstone standing proud on the east side.

"I almost didn't make it. Sorry I'm late," Mo said. He sat down facing Catarina's plaque, placed his bag on the stone and loosened his tie. He frowned. It had been too close and now he only had ten minutes before the cemetery closed. He'd worked as quickly as he could, but in his line of work, mistakes were fatal.

"You'll never believe what happened today." Mo laughed as the constriction in his chest eased now that he hadn't missed talking to her. How could the hospital be so busy two weeks in a row? Since last Saturday, he hadn't been on time to see Catarina, and an emergency call-in for work prevented him from coming on Sunday. At least it was Thursday now, and he was not on call this weekend. "Remember little Chloe? The girl with leukaemia? We found a match." Mo shook his head, still in disbelief over their luck.

"She's twelve now, and so cheeky—a beauty too. She might steal me away from you, you know. Anyway, the match is perfect. Provided everything goes well, this bone marrow transplant will save her life."

Mo blew away the dust from the stone, stroked Catarina's face on the photo there and told her about his day, beginning with how Ben's morning went. "He's growing so much and doesn't stop talking. He reminds me so much of you with his incessant energy."

"Sorry, Mo, we have to close."

"Okay, Mr Fletcher," Mo answered the old caretaker.

"I'll see you tomorrow. Hopefully, the hospital will be back to normal busy instead of the current insane level. So I can spend more time with you. Goodnight." Feet dragging, he forced himself down the path to the gate, appreciating the trees and the beautiful scent of flowers that would make

Catarina happy.

"Goodnight, Mr Fletcher," he said as he passed.

"See you tomorrow." The caretaker was already locking the gate behind him.

Mo walked towards his mum's house, his long legs eating up the pavement. That tightness across his chest returned as he wracked his brain for ways to make more time to visit Catarina. He couldn't leave patients before he'd finished seeing them, and he couldn't stop emergencies either. No matter how much he hated curtailing his daily thirty minutes with Catarina, he couldn't do anything about it. He'd have to stay longer at the weekends.

"Hello," he called out when he arrived.

"Hi, Dad." His four-year-old son, Ben, rushed out of the kitchen waving his hands. "Guess what I'm making."

"Bolinhos?" he asked in Portuguese—little cakes. One of his favourite desserts.

"How did you know?"

Mo laughed and picked Ben up, ruffling his mop of short curly hair. "I can smell them."

"Don't even think about it," Mum said, her back to them as she removed another batch of fried little cakes from the sizzling pan.

"I was only going to take one," Mo complained, eyeing the bowl of fragrant cakes on the table.

"I had one, Daddy. It was yummy."

Mo growled at Ben. "I bet it was. Shall I take it away from your tummy?" He poked and tickled until Ben was wriggling to get away.

"How was your day, Mum?" Mo asked when Ben escaped.

"I went to see Father Thomas. He asked after you."

Mo crossed his arms and fixed his gaze on his mum. "How is he?"

She carried on putting the next batch of cakes in the pan, her expression relaxed. "He's okay. It's been so long since he's seen you, and he's getting old, you know."

It had been four years since Mo last saw Father Thomas when he performed Catarina's funeral. The man had seemed old to Mo for all the twenty-eight years he could remember attending church. Father Thomas had performed Mo's baptism, holy communion, confirmation and marriage to Catarina, and Mo liked him. It was just the priest's boss, God, whom Mo hadn't gotten along with over the last few years.

"I'm glad he's okay. Was everything alright at school?" Mo asked, hoping to change the subject. His mum was doing what she thought was best for him, trying to get him to return to church, but he wasn't ready for that yet—didn't know if he ever would be.

His mum sighed. She knew better than to say anything more, but the reprieve would be temporary. She never gave up on what, in her opinion, was good for her children. Just like she hadn't given up on finding Mo a date, even though he'd told her he wasn't interested. Mo skated under the radar while his mum's attention focused on Noah, but now his eldest brother was engaged; her attention had turned to him.

"Ben's class went to the library today. He was grinning when he came out holding his book, so excited to show it to me that he couldn't keep it in his bag." Mo's mum shook her head, her straight black hair brushing the tops of her shoulders, her soft-brown eyes crinkling. "It's Mother's Reading Day next week."

"Are you still okay to go?"

"I can't wait. I'm beginning to think I wasted my time in nursing. I adore reading to those little kids."

Mo laughed. "Thanks, Mum." He didn't know what he'd do without his mother. Initially, childcare had been less of an issue. Ben went to nursery full-time, and his grandmother picked him up and cared for him until Mo finished work. But last September, the local school offered Ben a morning placement. Although Mo had planned on leaving Ben in a private nursery until he was four and could attend school full-time, Grandma had come to the rescue, taking Ben to the school nursery in the mornings and keeping him from lunchtime when it finished.

***

Beautiful memories flooded Shereen as she drove through the familiar streets of her hometown. Sometimes she wondered how she'd managed to stay away for so long. Pushing away old memories that had no business resurfacing when she should be worried about her mother, she parked outside her parents' house and rushed to the door.

"Hi Dad," Shereen said to the tall man who stood on the other side, ready to welcome her. She couldn't tell if his hair was greyer, but it definitely showed in his beard, and his face seemed sunken. She hugged him tightly, breathing in the slight scent of musk and cigarettes that never abandoned him. *How overwhelmed he must feel.* "I'm here to help now. How's Mum?" She pushed herself away from him and moved towards the stairs.

"Shh, she's just fallen asleep. We only got back from the hospital a couple of hours ago, and she's exhausted." Her dad pointed to the sitting room.

With an exaggerated tiptoe that had her dad stifling a snort of laughter, Shereen changed direction, her eyes searching for her mother the moment she entered the room. Sitting in the armchair beside the sofa, Shereen gazed at her mum, comforted to observe the gentle rise and fall of her chest. She could forgive anyone witnessing her current peaceful position for thinking her mother possessed a quiet temperament. The truth was Rosa Beckley was a force of nature.

Shereen's hand reached out to touch a cheek, but she pulled back, fearful of waking her. There were bruises on the soft mottled-brown skin on her face and arms. It was too hard to see her mother like that, and tears threatened. At a shuffle by the door, Shereen noted her dad's haggard appearance again. She blinked them away, then stood to link her arm with his and headed towards the kitchen, determined to cheer them both.

"I'll make coffee and something to eat." She pushed him into a chair by the kitchen table.

"You've been driving for hours. Let me make you something."

"I'm fine, Dad. I'm way younger than you, remember?" By the time Shereen was born, her mum and dad had given up on having children. After a bout of illness, her mum finally went to the doctor, who informed her she was five months pregnant. Though well into their forties with busy lives in academia, Shereen's parents could not have been happier at the news.

Her dad threw back his head and laughed, then quickly shoved his hand over his mouth. "That joke never grows old," he whispered. "It's so good to see you, sweetheart."

"You see me every day!"

"Arrgh," he scoffed. "Facetime is not the same as seeing you in person." He watched as she made coffee using the super-duper machine standing proudly on the kitchen worktop. "Rebecca brought food over this morning before I picked up your mum. It's in the fridge."

"That's nice, and so like I remember Auntie Rebecca." Rebecca had been a second mum to Shereen, the number of times she'd cared for her after school. Even when Shereen was old enough to stay home by herself, she'd spent all her weekdays after school and some weekends playing and eating dinner next door. As Rebecca's girls were older, she'd spent the most time with the boys, especially Mo, who was in her class. "What did the doctors say?"

"Your mum needs rest for a few weeks, but there's no long-term damage. She was lucky. She could easily have broken her hip."

"That's good, isn't it?"

"Yes, but she's so damn stubborn. I told her not to go to the rally. She's getting too old for them. But she wouldn't listen."

Shereen hugged him. She knew how her mum could be. But she'd also grown up witnessing her prepare for rallies across the country and fight passionately for equal rights. Being an activist was her mum's life. Age wasn't going to stop her.

"What if mum retired from rallying and stayed home to knit you cardigans and scarves? How would you feel?"

Her dad wrinkled his nose in disgust.

This time Shereen had to stifle her own laugh. "As much as you worry, you love her the way she is, stubborn and snarky."

After reheating and serving Rebecca's rice and chicken, Shereen sat at the table with her father. "I've missed this," she said after swallowing her first bite. Then she closed her eyes and chewed more slowly, savouring the tasty flavours, before forking another bite.

"Did you tell Mo you were coming?"

Shereen carried on eating slowly. "No. Should I have?"

Her dad's eyebrows lifted. "Why not? Did you fall out?"

"I don't tell Mo everything, you know." Standing, she walked towards the fridge and pulled out the jar of filtered cold water. "He's so busy, but I talk to him now and then."

Her dad savoured his mouthful of food, too, before responding. "That's good. You've always been such good friends."

Shereen hoped it would stay that way too.

She never wanted to stop being best friends with Mo Rodrigo. Their years together through primary and secondary school were her most precious memories. She would not allow the crush she'd had for him when she was fifteen to jeopardise that. It was her secret, and one Shereen had kept for seventeen years and intended to do so for the rest of her life. No way would she allow their relationship to become awkward because of her. Besides, she'd moved on from Mo a long time ago, so it would be best all around for it to remain a secret.

"Why didn't you tell me straight away that Mum had a fall?" she accused to change the subject.

Her dad sighed. "Darling, you know your mum. She insisted you had to meet your deadline."

"Dad! You– "

He held up a hand to stop her protest. "You know how proud she is of your career, even though she was initially disappointed you didn't follow our footsteps. She's accepted your choice to write and always brags about you to her friends. She said deadlines are important, and she wasn't going to be the reason you didn't meet yours."

"Dad, I can understand that, but can you see my point of view? Mum was in the hospital, and I wasn't there for her—or you." She appealed to his sense of fairness because she knew there was no point speaking to her mum about this. Her dad had always been able to listen to both sides of an argument and was, therefore, more likely to empathise with an opponent. However, it was almost impossible to change her mum's mind. "Yes, my career is important, and so are deadlines. But you're both more important than work."

"And your fans? Wouldn't they have anything to say about not getting the next Alex Caddell instalment on the day it's due?"

Shereen glared, then noticed his worried look. "Dad, I was scared."

"I know, honey. But you know, no matter what your mother says, I'd have called straight away if I thought there was any danger. This injury was more an insult to her pride rather than anything dangerous."

Shereen knew he was right. When it mattered most, he'd always stood up to Mum.

"So, you've sent over your manuscript?" he asked with a playful smile.

Shereen got the message. He'd said his piece and was ready to change the subject. She'd just have to trust him. With time her heart would calm, and she'd go back to being anxiety-free as her mum got back to her usual everyday activities.

"Yes. It's with my editor now."

"When is the book out?"

"Early next year."

"That's such a long time to wait. I finished the last one ages ago."

Shereen laughed. "You're worse than my fans, Dad."

"What do you mean? I'm your number one fan!"

Shereen laughed harder. Her dad had always been able to make her laugh. Both of her parents had, but more so as she got older and understood their sense of humour better.

"How long can you stay? You haven't been home in nearly two years." He looked hopeful.

"I'll stay a few months. I've brought my laptop and notes, so I'll work from here for a while. I want to make sure Mum is okay before I return to Leeds. My publisher doesn't care where I work from as long as I'm getting the work done."

"Well, now you're here, I'll get to read a little about the book before it goes out," he hinted.

"You're my number one fan. Remember? So you get my books when other fans do."

"Spoilsport," her Dad said, but there was a smile in his eyes, and he looked more relaxed than when she arrived.

Shereen opened the door to the garden and spied the swing her dad had built when she was four. It was special because of the time she'd spent there with the Rodrigo boys but also because it was rare that her father made anything. He'd always joked he was no good with his hands.

In the left corner of the garden, there was a tiny treehouse her dad had paid a carpenter to build. Whenever she wasn't at the Rodrigo's, that's where she'd be, usually with her nose in a book.

"I'll help take your things upstairs." Her dad put their empty plates in the sink.

"I'll do the dishes when I come down." She followed him to the hallway, pulled her luggage out of his hands and stumbled upstairs. She pushed open her bedroom door and wrestled the suitcase into the room with purple walls. *Gosh, the taste I had when I was a teenager*. Her bedroom was precisely as she left it before moving to Leeds University fourteen years ago. She'd come home for Christmas in the first few years, but the summers she'd worked or travelled. She'd never stayed long enough to change the decor. That would change this time around. It was time to move on from her childhood and paint her room a more modern colour.

She spied Fluto on her pillow and picked him up.

"Hi, you. How have you been?" She hugged the soft purple elephant. Warmth radiated from him, easing her tension. How was that possible? Then she realised the sun had been shining in through the window right on his spot on the bed.

"There you go." Her dad came in and gently put her laptop bag and work tote on the floor beside the bed. He pointed at Fluto. "He still looks brand new. Didn't Mo win that for you at that fair when you were about fifteen?"

Shereen looked up at him. Sometimes, a look or a comment made her wonder if her dad had known about her crush on Mo. "He did, but it went so well with the decorations that it was a shame to put it away." She placed Fluto back on the bed. "I'm going to paint the room white so he won't match anymore. I'll probably end up giving him away. I'm sure someone somewhere can give him some love.

Dad nodded.

"Leave the dishes; I'll do them," Shereen said again, then quickly stowed her suitcase and followed him. He was bound to do the dishes if she didn't get to them first. But, she also needed to get away from the memories that room held. Beautiful, wonderful and sad memories she wanted to stuff back in the recesses of her mind, but as they flooded out, they seemed to expand and no longer fit.

Shereen loved the older version of her parents. Since retiring from teaching at their respective universities, they had time to talk, enjoy a leisurely meal together and watch TV or play games.

What a shame that now they had more time to spend with her; she was far away.

I've missed home. So why have I stayed away for so long?

Chapter 2

Mo smiled. Ben was standing on a stool washing his hands at the kitchen sink. He was so good at getting ready and sometimes seemed much older than four. But Ben missed having a mum. Mo could see it in the way Ben watched children with their mothers when they were at the park and even when watching movies.

Ben got down, dried his hands, then grabbed his belongings and kissed his grandmother. "Tell Grandad I'll see him tomorrow."

The doorbell rang. Mo couldn't suppress a smile when he opened the door to his long-time friend Shereen Beckley. Stepping outside, he wrapped his arms around Shereen and lifted her off the ground, spinning while she laughed.

"Put me down, you big oaf."

"What did you just say?" Mo twirled a couple more times before setting her down.

"You're an oaf. I can't believe you've got even

more muscles. Shouldn't you have stopped growing by now?"

"Jealous much?"

"What, of your good looks? And height?" Shereen stood on her slipper-clad tiptoes. "I've grown too. We're nearly the same height."

Mo gave her ponytail a playful tug and slapped his hand on top of her head, pushing her back down, then bringing his palm across to the base of his neck, he measured them. "I'm a whole head taller."

"No need to rub it in."

"You're the one who's always been bothered you weren't growing tall enough to compete with me. Remember that time I finally overtook you and was an inch taller when your dad measured us? You sulked for at least a week."

Shereen play-tapped the side of his head.

"Ouch," Mo complained, rubbing at the spot.

"I was six! Besides, we'd pretty much been head-to-head until that time. It was a big shock. We were just starting year three, and I was so proud of being one of the tallest children in our class. I went from being the joint tallest to second place. It was a big deal at the time. Especially because I wanted to show that Harry twerp, that girls were just as tall, clever and strong as boys."

Ben tugged at Mo's trouser leg, so he bent to

pick him up. "Hey, Ben, do you remember Auntie Shereen?" Ben's eyes were wide as he looked at Shereen.

"Ben, you've grown too." Shereen leaned in and kissed his soft brown cheek. Mo caught a whiff of her familiar perfume and smiled at the memory.

"I'm as tall as your knees," Ben declared.

Mo put him down again. "Let's see." As he'd just done between them, Mo measured Ben's height against Shereen's legs.

"Wow, Ben, you are. I think you're going to be taller than your dad," she gushed, earning a smile from Ben.

"That's cool. Then I can do grown-up things like Dad."

Shereen canted her head. "What grown-up things?"

Mo placed his hand on Ben's shoulders and gently turned him away from Shereen. "It's bedtime for someone who's not a grown-up yet. Say bye to Auntie Shereen. See you tomorrow, Mum," Mo called out as his mum approached the door.

"We'll have to catch up while you're here, Shereen," Mo said from the car. "No excuses about how busy you are. And don't let Mum browbeat you into doing jobs for her."

He enjoyed Shereen's laugh. It had been a while since he'd heard it.

"I've come on an errand for my mum. She's the one that wants the help. I'll call you once I've finished sorting out a few things." Shereen waved in his rearview mirror with his mum smiling beside her as Mo pulled out of the driveway.

Ben waved back until a large tree hid them. "I like Auntie Shereen," he told Mo, busy looking out for different coloured cars.

"She's nice," Mo agreed, thinking how much their lives had changed since their school days together, yet now they barely saw each other. Sure, they FaceTimed a couple of times a month, and he'd thought that was enough. But seeing her in person made Mo realise how much he'd missed her living next door to his parents. There was something different about the Shereen he'd just seen, though, and his brow furrowed as he tried to pinpoint what exactly had changed.

"I spy a red van. One point to me, Daddy."

Mo shook his head and focused on the game he always played with Ben. This week's goal was to spot the most red vans and whoever did so was the winner. A few minutes later, Mo pulled into a small driveway outside a charming three-bedroom house. He'd bought it with Catarina when they found out she was pregnant.

Though they'd both loved their flat in Central London, which was a short walk to their respective hospitals, the shops and cafes they frequented, they both wanted to raise their children closer to family. This house had plenty of room in the back garden for an extension in the future and was near both their parents' homes, a good school and the train station.

Mo left his bag by the entrance, kicked off his shoes and headed for the stairs, as Ben did the same.

"Come on, little boy, it's time for your bath."

Ben giggled. "I'm not little, Daddy. Auntie Shereen said I'm big."

Mo laughed. "Not so big that I can't carry you."

"On your shoulders, Daddy?"

"Not in the house where you can bang your head. Piggyback?" Mo suggested and crouched for Ben to jump up and secure his arms and legs around him. Ben chuckled as he ran up the stairs, making train noises. Then laughed as they squeezed through the doorway. "Mind the gap!"

"Get undressed. I'll run the bath."

As he sat on the edge of the bathtub, Mo marvelled at the bright white and blue bathroom Catarina had decorated *and filled with far too many bath toys,* he thought as he tipped the lot into the water. As always, Catarina had gone overboard and bought too many.

"Just in case," was what she always said to justify her purchases. Plucking up a blue duck, he caressed it, imagining Catarina's fingers brushing over the same spot to assess how soft it would be. A vivid image of her in the shop popped into his mind, her huge eyes closed and lips turned up in bliss at the beautiful sensation of the duck.

"Don't forget my bubbles," Ben pulled him out of the memory. "I'm ready, Dad."

Mo reached for the bottle, glancing at his son. "Hey, clothes in the hamper, remember?"

"Keep your hair on," Ben giggled as he picked up his discarded clothes.

"Keep my hair on?" Mo laughed, tickling Ben's sides before lifting him into the tub. "In you go." Ben played with the toys and the bubbles while Mo grabbed a flannel to help him wash.

"I can do it myself." Ben took the washcloth.

"Okay, big man. Keep your hair on," Mo teased before praising Ben. "You're doing a great job."

Ben's right cheek dimple stood out as his lips lifted. "You're going to be proud of me."

"I already am. What did you do today?"

Mo listened as Ben told him what had happened during his day, washing all the places Ben forgot and rinsing his hair with the shower head attachment. He loved hearing his son talk, enjoying the anecdotes and drama of nursery school life. But as crucial for Mo was keeping his promise to Catarina who had spoken of listening to their child and loving them as a person. She had planned to understand what their child thought and wanted to do in life.

“All squeaky clean,” Mo announced, lifting Ben out, and wrapping him up in a large blue towel.

“I can put the cream on too, Dad.”

“What am I going to do if you can bathe all by yourself?” Mo made a sad face and pretended to cry.

Ben hugged his legs. “Don’t cry, Daddy. You can wash the toys. They still need help, and you can read to me. It takes me too long—” Ben spread his arms, “to read a whole bedtime story.”

“Go put on your pyjamas then, and I’ll see to my cleaning duties,” Mo grumbled, spraying down the toys that were spiralling the drain and washing away the last of the bubbles. Then he lined them up along the back edge of the bath in height order, just as Catarina had left them.

By the time Mo had hung up the wet towel to dry, Ben was tucked up in his bed talking to his favourite worn-out teddy bear. Mo picked up a storybook. He smiled at his sleeping son halfway through, put away the book and switched off the light.

Grabbing a beer from the fridge and some snacks from a cupboard, Mo headed for the sitting room. He flexed his neck and shoulders before picking up the DVD player remote and hitting play.

"What do you think of your crib, Pea? Doesn't Mummy have great taste?" Catarina asked from the TV screen, brown-black eyes smiling. She'd left her hair down that day, and the black curls gracefully framed her heart-shaped face—she glowed in the third trimester of her pregnancy.

"What do you mean, great taste—blue everything? As long as it's blue, it's beautiful?" Mo asked out of shot. Then he appeared on the screen. "Pea, you'll be grateful your daddy was here when Mummy was choosing your cot. Otherwise, you'd get a blue cot. And if you're a girl, you might hate everything blue, right? Mummy's a bit weird that way. She's just lucky I love her anyway, and you will too."

"Daddy's silly, isn't he? You'll soon get to see how silly he can be." Catarina shook her head. "Anyway, I wanted you to see Mummy and Daddy buying your cot. I know you'll just love it. Bye for now." She waved at the camera.

"Bye, kiddo," he said, waving too.

Mo paused the screen on the frame of the two of them waving, their bodies touching. That was a rare day when neither of them was on call. They'd started getting all the baby stuff early in her pregnancy whenever their schedules allowed, so by the time Catarina was seven months, only the cot was left. Mo recalled the beautiful summer's day, and after shopping, they'd gone to Mo's favourite restaurant. It had been his turn to choose where they ate, and Mo refused to forfeit, knowing Catarina only pretended she didn't enjoy the brown beans served there.

He missed her laugh, her smile and the way she wouldn't stop talking. How she'd go to work excited and come back in the evening still full of energy. But most of all, he missed her touch.

"You can't live without touch," Catarina had often joked with him. "If you were the only man left on earth, you'd die not of hunger or any dangerous animals but from lack of touch. Your nickname should be cat, not mine."

Mo had often laughed it off, but he was dying from the lack of her touch day by day. He missed her warmth beside him when they sat on the sofa together, watching the videos she filmed of their family, the pregnancy vlog for Ben, films of surgeries and occasionally a movie. They even sat together when they were reading medical journals they loved.

He touched the empty seat beside him on the large brown leather sofa. It had taken him forever to convince Catarina they should buy it. She'd loved the design but had wanted it in blue. They already had so much blue in their house, and Mo had to put his foot down. "You can always put blue cushions on it," he'd suggested.

Catarina had agreed, conceding she had, after all, vowed to compromise sometimes. That was the endearing thing about his wife. She loved having her own way, but if you stood up for yourself and gave her a convincing argument, she'd backed down quickly.

Mo sighed and went to grab another beer. He checked his phone and smiled at a missed call from Tae Joon. He dealt with his other messages, then dialled his friend's number.

"You know I can't come clubbing with you tonight," Mo said when his call connected.

"I know. I just needed a distraction," Tae Joon answered.

"How is it going?"

"Not so good. It's boring without you. We had so much fun last time you came. None of the other guys can put away the drink as well as you."

Mo laughed. "I'm still not coming. Ben is asleep now."

"Is that the only reason? I know Mrs Rodrigo would love to babysit her youngest grandson. And he'd love sleeping over. Ben always does."

The sound of music increased, and Mo stared at the can of beer he'd grabbed. "Tae Joon, go have yourself some fun. I'm hanging up. See you at football on Saturday."

Mo headed back to the sofa. At first, he'd been

annoyed when his family and friends started setting him up. It had hurt him that they couldn't see his vows to Catarina still mattered, even in death. The promise he'd made to her that she was the only woman for him was a promise he wanted to keep for the rest of his life.

Mo understood his mum's point of view. He was her son, and she worried about him and her grandson, who she wanted to grow up with a mother. With children of their own, his sisters had a similar perspective. It was the thoughtless actions of his single brothers and friends, trying to set him up or use him as a wingman, that angered him at first. Now, though it still frustrated him sometimes, he'd come to see they cared for him. Instead, he'd found better ways to avoid blind dates, even from his crafty mum. But since Noah and Libby got engaged, his mum had stepped up her game. It'd been hell these last few months avoiding all the subtle ways she had found to get him alone with a woman she thought he'd like, who would make a nice mother for Ben.

Keeping his promise to Catarina was as much about loving and preserving her memory as it was the type of man he wanted to be. It wasn't Catarina's fault she'd died, and just because she'd passed, it didn't mean she was no longer the only woman in his life. Yes, it was hard not having her physical presence beside him every day. Hell, he was as healthy as any other thirty-two-year-old man, but just like any married or committed man out there who had to live without his partner for a while, it'd be wrong to cheat. The only difference between him and those other men was that his wait might be a few decades. It didn't matter. He'd have to have the same self-discipline.

Pressing the remote, he started the next video on the DVD filmed in the first year of their marriage.

Chapter 3

"Me?" Shereen asked Rebecca, eyes wide.

"You don't think you can do it?" Rebecca looked at Shereen's mum and dad. "I know you can do it perfectly well, and Ben will have more fun with you. All that youthful energy."

Her mum touched Shereen's shoulder. "You'll be a wonderful babysitter."

Rebecca looked at Shereen. "It's okay if you can't. But I wanted to ask while your mum and dad were here because it might interfere with you helping your mum out."

"Nonsense!" her mum said, a marshalling light entering her eyes. "You know how I hate being fussed over. I've been home for five days and can mostly manage by myself. Besides, Andy is here." She leaned into Shereen's dad, and he squeezed her.

"It's a great idea," he confirmed.

Shereen gazed at them, dumbfounded. It

wasn't that she'd never babysat. She'd just never done it on her own. She was an only child, and both her parents' families abandoned them when her white dad married her beautiful, black mum.

She reminded herself she'd played with lots of young children and helped babysit next door. She was ahead enough in her work that she could take a break. Apart from keeping her parents company and occasionally helping Mum to and from the bathroom, she didn't have much to do. She'd done most of the urgent jobs she had to do her first few days in London. Besides, with Ben at school a couple of hours each morning, it only left the afternoons when she'd have to care for him. Mum and Dad were happy for her to do it, so that left only one question?

"Did you check Mo was alright with it?"

Auntie Rebecca shook her head. "Mo trusts you. He'd be thrilled with you taking care of Ben. But you know him. If I asked, he'd worry about imposing upon you and end up getting a childminder. I'd rather Ben was with family, which you are in my book. The first time the church asked me to go on this trip I refused, because of Ben. Zacchaeus was going to go on his own. But since you're here and Ben loves you, I thought to myself, why not ask Shereen."

"I'd love to do it," Shereen finally conceded. She wanted to help Mo out, and she couldn't say no to his mother. Auntie Rebecca meant too much to her, and she couldn't deprive Uncle Zac of a trip with his wife. After their hard lives and the recent death of Auntie Rebecca's brother, Seb, Mo's parents deserved all the happiness they could get.

"Thank you, Shereen. Your uncle and I really appreciate this. He would be fine on his own, but you know I like to check everything myself."

Oh, how Shereen knew. Auntie Rebecca was a true matriarch, excelling at delegating her family or members of the church. She and Uncle were in charge of the gift aid contributions for the church they attended, which had set up this excursion. People like themselves would learn how to improve the services they oversaw. They'd only be away for five school days.

"It's up to you which of our houses you use to spend time with Ben but here might not be such a good idea because of your mum."

Mum coughed. "Rebecca, I love you and your help, but we're going to fall out if you keep making me seem like some senile invalid."

Rebecca laughed, her eyes crinkling. "Alright then. It's just as well you don't get sick often." She looked at Shereen's dad. "I think this is the first time I've known you to be seriously ill in the thirty or so years we've known each other."

Dad was laughing too, "She's unbearable when she's ill."

"I'm leaving before she throws something at me." Rebecca stood up. "Shereen, do you have time to pick up Ben with me today so you meet his teacher? I'm afraid all your old teachers left. They were so nice too."

"Don't you like Ben's teacher?" Dad asked.

"I do, she's lovely, and Ben likes her. It's just a little sad seeing teachers leave. But I guess it'd be a bit too much to expect your old teachers to be there. I'm just nostalgic, I guess."

"What time shall I come over?"

"Quarter to twelve. Ben finishes at five past, so that gives us plenty of time to get there. Take care, Rosa and Andy."

After Rebecca left, Shereen went up to her bedroom and lay there thinking about how her days would change next week while taking care of Ben.

***

Shereen pushed her hair behind her ears and adjusted the strap of her bag. She was way too early for picking up Ben, but luckily, a few adults were dotted around the playground, to collect kids from other classes. Besides, the gates opened ten minutes before collection time, so she was only ten minutes early by her reckoning.

She looked about the school, noting the climbing frame and wood around the tree in the middle of the playground. The school looked bigger and better than when she'd been a pupil there—more classrooms and all the walls painted bright green and orange.

She'd been happy at Richard Addison Primary, running in the playground with Mo and their friends and enjoying the plays they'd put on for Christmas. Occasionally, a few of the boys had teased her—she was tall, wore thick glasses and could be moody. Mo would soon tell them where to get off, and when she wanted to sit by herself, he'd be right there with her, saying nothing. When they were older, Mo seemed to read her moods and ask if her parents had argued. It never surprised her he had become such a good doctor.

Others picking up children from Ben's class soon joined Shereen, so she felt less conspicuous. She spied Ben in the classroom, sitting on the floor, listening attentively to whatever the teacher said. He sat precisely in the way Mo had done when they were in school that she couldn't help but smile.

"Auntie Shereen!" Ben shouted as he ran towards her.

She caught him in a bear hug, enjoying his energy and happiness. "Did you have a good day?"

"Our rabbit had babies. They're teeny tiny. Mrs May said we couldn't pet Molly because she might be sensitive."

Shereen smiled when Ben tripped over the long word. She'd struggled with words, too, until she was five.

"But we can pet her next week. Isn't that wonderful?"

"It sounds like fun."

Ben tucked his hand in hers as Shereen began walking home, adjusting her step to his, dodging buggies and other children milling about the playground.

Ben continued talking about his morning while swinging his free arm. He looked so cute with his little backpack that Shereen was having difficulty stopping herself from hugging him again. She had always loved children and never could contain her joy at being with them. Whenever her friend Sophie visited, Shereen would carry her baby daughter all the time. "You'll spoil her," Sophie would say before replacing her in her car seat.

"What are we having for lunch?"

"Sausage and mash. Do you like that?"

"That's my favourite! How did you know? Did Daddy tell you?"

Shereen laughed. "We're going to eat at my house with my mum and dad. Is that okay?"

Ben nodded. "I've been there lots and eaten with Mr and Mrs Beckley lots too."

"You have?" Shereen knew Mo had helped her

parents with occasional errands, and she remembered Dad mentioned he had watched Ben for Mo because of an emergency, but she didn't know Ben ate with them.

"Sometimes Daddy has dinner with them too, and once, we went out to eat all together.

"I bet your Daddy was helping my parents. He's good at helping people."

"My dad's the best. Uncle Noah too. Nana says she brought 'em up right." Ben's imitation of Rebecca had Shereen letting out a snorting laugh.

Arriving home, Shereen warned Ben to be gentle with her mum and watched as he slowly approached. Then, after carefully greeting her with two kisses, he charged at her dad, who picked him up, swinging him high. Surprised at how familiar they were with each other, Shereen crossed her arms, fascinated by how her father lit up in Ben's presence.

"I'm going to set the table," she said when she began feeling a little jealous of their apparent friendship.

"I'll help. I set the table, and Mrs Beckley dishes the food."

"Let's wash our hands first." Shereen walked to the kitchen sink and lifted Ben so he could wash his hands.

"I'll set the table with Ben," her dad said, taking his turn with the soap.

He took out a tablecloth, gave one side of it to Ben and together, they put it on the table. Shereen watched them push and pull the cloth, trying to get it even. Her dad deliberately messing it up and making Ben giggle. She shook her head, a smile playing on her mouth.

She started dishing up the food, which was her dad's cue to move things on, placing cutlery, glasses and condiments. Shereen took the full plates to the table, navigating around Ben.

Her mum let out a laugh.

"Is it so much fun watching us slaving while you sit prettily on the couch, Rosa?" her dad asked with a pretend put-out face, hands on his hips.

Ben mimicked him.

Mum laughed again, a strange faraway expression on her face. "You two reminded me of when I was a little girl. My brothers, sisters and I would mess around setting the table like that."

Shereen stopped serving and looked at her mum, surprised because she hardly talked about her family. Shereen had asked plenty of times, especially when she was little and wished for cousins. But, as she grew older, she'd learned it wasn't worth upsetting her mum when it never garnered her any answers. Everything little Shereen knew about her mother's family had come from her dad.

Ben canted his head. “Do you have lots of brothers and sisters, Mrs Beckley?”

Shereen’s mum nodded. “I have two brothers and two sisters.” But then Shereen noticed a sad look came over her face. “I’m hungry, and the food’s ready. Let’s eat.”

“Shall we help Mrs Beckley?” her dad asked Ben, and they walked over to the sofa, and her dad helped her mum up. Ben carried her mum’s cushion, and together they walked the short distance to the table, with her mum hobbling on her crutches.

Shereen turned away and breathed deeply. She was used to Mum not talking about her family. But even though it had hurt when she was younger, she now understood why it was hard for her.

“Can you cut up your sausages, or shall I help you?” Shereen asked Ben.

“No, thank you.” He picked up his knife and fork and started cutting up a sausage and eating slowly. Shereen was impressed, though it took him a while, and his food sloshed around.

Shereen patted his head. “Well done. You’re good at cutting.”

Ben nodded, his mouth stuffed with sausage and mash.

“And you know you don’t talk with your mouth full too.”

Ben looked at Shereen as if that was a silly comment to make.

He finished chewing and swallowed. "I knew that when I was two years old. It's gross to eat with your mouth open. Dad and Nana taught me that and how to use a knife and fork too." He gulped some water. "Dad said I had to learn or I couldn't go to school."

Shereen coughed into her elbow. She was having a hard time trying not to laugh. Ben was just so cute.

"Well done. When I was your age, I couldn't cut up my food."

"That's true, Ben," Dad said, shaking his head.

"It took you a long time to learn, didn't it? Andy, was Shereen four or five before she could use a knife and fork without half her food falling on the table?"

Ben looked from Shereen to her parents, eyes huge.

"Five," Dad answered.

Those had been awful moments, Shereen recalled. It had been a struggle, and of course, they teased her at school about how such a big girl couldn't use a knife and fork properly. She'd even asked her parents for a packed lunch instead of having school dinners because she'd been so embarrassed. Now, that memory brought up a fact she thought to share with Ben.

"Your dad used to help cut up my food. I would eat all the food that didn't need cutting and then push the meat around until the other kids played outside. He would stay behind and cut it up for me."

"He did?"

Shereen nodded. "He was just as good as you at cutting up his food when he was your age."

Ben smiled.

"I have to say," her mum added, "Mo has always been a great friend to you."

Shereen looked at the odd expression on her mother's face. Just what was she implying. Her dad was nodding too.

"Shereen, do you remember when you were ten or eleven and fell over, hurting your knee? It was just before you started secondary school." Her dad recalled. "Mo carried you all the way home on his back. I was working from home that day and can still remember the shock when I opened the door. Your tear-stained face was peeking over Mo's shoulder as he did his best to avoid hurting your poor knee."

"Yes," her mum picked up the story thread, "When I came home, Shereen, you were in your bed. I'd gone next door to fetch you, and Rebecca told me what happened."

"My dad carried you on his back? But you were the same age!" Ben's eyes were bulging again.

Dad spoke before Shereen could utter a word. "Your dad was taller than Auntie Shereen by then and so strong."

Shereen's look to her parents was incredulous. Why were they going down memory lane like this? She wasn't that embarrassed in front of Ben, but she didn't' want the boy reminding Mo of those cringy moments.

She turned to Ben, aiming to distract his thoughts so he would forget what he'd heard. "Ben, what shall we do this afternoon? How about a visit to the park?" Shereen shot warning glances at her parents. "I think there are lots of new slides and swings, aren't there?"

"Oh, yes, the park! The park! There's a new, really high climbing frame. I climb right to the top, and I'm not scared."

"Okay, that's decided. We'll go to the park." Shereen smiled, satisfied his enthusiasm overtook his curiosity of her childhood with his dad. Deliberately, she ignored the knowing smiles that passed between her parents. Mo didn't need reminders of those few silly moments. All kids had some issues, and hers resolved as she grew up into a strong and perfectly average child.

"What shall we do after we come back from the park?" Shereen asked, not wanting the conversation to lull back into nostalgia.

Ben started to name games he liked to play, and her parents suggested twister and even scrabble, which was too old for Ben. Shereen let them carry on, glad her parents had given up reminiscing about her somewhat quirky childhood.

***

Mo looked at Toby's eyes, noting the increasing yellow around the boy's irises. But, at the moment, he could do little about the jaundice.

"The bone marrow transplant will resolve that, and your eyes will be white again. How is school?" He asked.

"It's okay. Sometimes the other children ask why my eyes are yellow. I don't like it," Toby mumbled, clearly embarrassed.

Mo nodded, sympathy filling his heart for this eleven-year-old boy who still tried to do all he could despite the obstacles in his way.

"Do your knees still hurt when you go swimming?"

"Yes," Toby answered, looking miserable.

Toby's mum spoke up, taking Mo's attention away from the boy. "I think it's getting worse. I make sure he rubs the Vicks into his legs, and I rub Vaseline on his back afterwards. They seem to help. I have the towel ready to go to make sure he's warmed up as soon as he gets out of the water." She paused. “Dr Rodrigo, is there anything else you can recommend that might help?”

Stopping swimming, especially in winter, was on the tip of Mo’s tongue to say, but he was loath to suggest that. Often children with sickle cell gave up so many activities because of their illness, and he didn’t want to advise Toby to stop doing something he enjoyed and was good at.

“Would it be feasible to have a warm drink ready? Also, you can try to make sure Toby stretches a little before he goes into the water. That might help. Some parents have reported rubbing Vicks on the back as well as the legs, instead of Vaseline, is more helpful.”

“We’ll try all of those then,” Toby’s mum said. “Right, Toby?”

“How did you do in the competition?” Mo asked.

“I won.” Toby’s happy smile almost reached ear to ear. “The silver medallist was very close, but I put a spurt on at the end and won.”

“That’s your first gold medal, isn’t it?” Mo tried to recall their past conversations. He’d been following Toby for a couple of years in the haematology clinic and had grown fond of him. For most of his childhood, his sickle cell anaemia had been well-controlled, but last year his Doppler scans, measuring the flow of blood in the brain, had shown he was at risk of a stroke. Unfortunately for

Toby, after starting fortnightly blood transfusion treatment for stroke prevention, he'd developed antibodies. This meant the treatment had to stop, and the only remaining viable option was a bone marrow transplant. It was costly and only offered on the national health service in exceptional circumstances like Toby's.

If Mo was honest with himself, he found it almost impossible not to be fond of his paediatric patients. "You've been swimming since you were five, if I remember correctly."

"That's right, Doctor," Toby answered. "I've been competing for about a year now, so it's great to win this medal."

"If there are no other questions, hop up onto the couch, and I'll check your tummy."

Toby lay down on the table across the room and lifted his shirt up. Mum stood by Toby's feet. Mo washed his hands in warm water at the sink in the room, dried them thoroughly and went to examine Toby's abdomen.

"Everything feels fine. Your spleen is a little distended, but not to a size that is even remotely worrying. I'll make a note of that, and we'll check it next time. When are your appointments for the MRI scan and lung function tests?"

"Next week, they are on the same day." Toby's mum replied.

Mo nodded. "Don't forget to keep taking your regular medication, as well as the new pre-transplant regimen."

"Toby's better at remembering now. We even leave the penicillin by his bed with a bottle of water. As soon as he wakes up, that's what he takes. By the time he's finished getting ready for school, and it's nearly time to leave, he has his breakfast."

"It's good you have a strategy. I know it's hard to remember the one hour before food rule. Next time you come, you can meet one of our previous transplant patients to chat with him. So think about any questions you might want to ask." Mo printed out a letter. "Hand this over at reception, and they'll book an appointment."

When they left, Mo finished typing up his notes then waited for his last patient, still thinking about Toby's family. None of Toby's siblings was a match, so Toby's mum was the donor. Although half-matches sometimes caused complications, their success rate increased the more they learned about them. Besides, the procedure with his mum as the donor was better than the possibility of no transplant.

"Come in," Mo said when a knock sounded.

A little girl of about seven, all large eyes and long hair, came in holding on to a man's hand. They looked so much alike that Mo thought this was Dad. Mo had met her only a few months ago, and on that occasion, she'd been with her mother.

"Hello, I'm Dr Rodrigo, a specialist haematologist doctor working under Dr Rodway. We haven't met. I saw Ellie last time she attended the clinic." He shook the man's hand before proceeding with the consultation.

After typing up Ellie's notes, Mo stretched and left the office to go and find his boss, Professor Rodway, a consultant paediatric haematologist. Though he was tired, Mo had never regretted his decision to extend his training beyond his haematology specialism. He loved paediatric haematology, and after a meeting with his boss, he checked on a couple of patients in the haematology day ward. Mo finished his long day going over an experiment in the lab, leaving the hospital by six and arriving at the cemetery half an hour later.

"Are you happy to see me on time, finally? It was a long day, but everything went as planned at least." Mo sat down by Catarina's headstone to talk to her about his day and how Ben was doing.

"I told you Shereen is taking care of Ben today, didn't I? I haven't had any calls, and no call is a good thing, right? Shereen has always loved children and once told me she wants to have six." Mo laughed. "I pity the man she ends up marrying. I like the sound of her current boyfriend; he seems like a good guy. Hopefully, she'll settle down and marry him, provided he's happy to have six little ones. I'll let you know how things went with her and Ben tomorrow."

Mo waved to the old caretaker, who was busy speaking with a family. They seemed like they were new at the cemetery, the way they looked lost and confused. Mo sighed and headed towards home. He'd never stop missing Catarina, and he knew the gaping hole she'd left would likely never be filled.

Sure, his life was much better than those first days and months after she passed. He couldn't even remember the first few days. He'd gone through the stages of grief everyone talked of, denying her death at first and hoping she'd come home. When it sunk in that wasn't going to happen, he'd spent a long time being numb and drinking to avoid the pain of her absence. To his profound shame, he'd even been unable to spend time with Ben. Whenever his mum or dad tried to get Mo to spend time with Ben, all he'd been able to see was that Ben's life meant Catarina's death. Thankfully, in time, Mo came to see the little boy he and Catarina had wanted and loved so much.

He remembered his promise to Catarina to take care of any children they had if anything ever happened to her. And do it well. Since then, he'd started spending time with Ben, at first at his parent's house for a few hours at a time. Eventually, when Ben was four months old, Mo had taken him home and never looked back. His son still reminded Mo of Catarina—his large brown-black eyes, how he laughed and especially his energy.

Catarina was still in his life through his visits to the cemetery and her videos. Mo spent his evenings and a good part of his weekends with her. She was the love of his life, as he promised her she always would be. However, it was becoming hard to ignore that he was lonely. He missed her touch like any husband who was apart from his wife would.

Mo adjusted his bag as he walked to his mum's house. When he found out Shereen would be taking care of Ben while his parents were away, an idea had entered his head that he couldn't shake. He would tell himself it was a silly thought, but a minute later, his thoughts would stray back to it. Could Shereen be the answer to his loneliness? Would she help him?

A friend of Mo's, who had been married for a year, cheated on his wife when she went to work abroad for a lengthy contract. They'd seemed alright at first with daily FaceTime chats and quarterly visits, but before the year was over, he'd betrayed her.

"I missed the sex. But most of all, I missed the touch of another human being," he replied when Mo had asked why he did it when he seemed to love his wife dearly.

And Mo understood. Even though he couldn't

condone it and would never have been able to hurt Catarina like that, loneliness was something he'd begun to recognise all too well. He was shocked at himself, even though it felt like he'd been without her touch forever, Catarina had passed only four years ago. He had to admit he was a little disappointed that he hadn't been able to last longer before loneliness dug its claws into him. He missed sex, but there wasn't a woman he wanted to be with that way. Even though he didn't believe he'd ever sleep with anyone, he missed someone's touch.

Maybe there was an appropriate way to fix his problem that even Catarina couldn't fault. That was where his friend Shereen came in. He and Shereen always had a platonic relationship where they could sit together and not feel anything the least bit sexual. He could hug her just like he was hugging one of his sisters, but it was somehow more personal than that. So the idea hovering in the back of his mind was spending time with Shereen. She said it herself. She was going to take a little holiday from work and would have some spare time. They had arranged to go out soon, but since she was taking care of Ben, could he tempt her to spend more time together?

The holidays were coming up, and he'd already planned a few days off work. If Shereen accepted, surely the time they spent together would help erase some of his loneliness? There'd never been a time he'd spent with Shereen when he hadn't felt happy and in a good headspace. The problem was he wasn't sure what to say to Shereen. Or if he should say anything at all. Surely they could be two friends spending time together. But somehow, Mo felt a friend would be open about the situation. But what could he say?

"Hi, Shereen, can you please spend a few days hanging out with me, as a friend, to cure my loneliness?" Geez, he even grossed himself out saying it that way. How could Shereen not be?

Chapter 4

Mo used his key to open the door to his mum's house. An unusual quiet greeted him, and with a frown, he slid off his shoes, placed his bag on the hallway table and padded to the kitchen–empty. As he walked through to the sitting room, he spotted them–Shereen and Ben, side by side and fast asleep. Ben had leaned over, his head resting on Shereen's side, her body almost protectively curved towards him. Mo stood transfixed at the beautiful sight of them sleeping, then it hit him, bowled him over like a bulldozer. That's what Ben wanted, needed even—a mum to play with him until they both tired themselves out; to hug him and tuck him into bed; to cook for him and listen to his chatter.

Mo blinked away the tears, tiptoeing to the back door for some air but knowing he could do nothing to relieve the anger inside. He wanted to punch someone or something. Taking a couple of steps to the kitchen wall, he rubbed his fisted knuckles over the rough brick, then stopped. Was he really going to punch the wall? It wouldn't be the first time but would be for the same reason—Catarina. He was over that, wasn't he? He recalled the pain of flesh against red-brick and stretched his hands to note the faint scarring from the self-inflicted damage. Instead, he breathed deeply and thought of Ben. His son needed a sane father who wasn't always mad with the world.

Stay mad with God.

He shook his head and made his way back into the kitchen. Reaching behind the tins of tuna and hot dogs in one cupboard, he found the key to his parent's secret stash of alcohol. Mo unlocked the bottom cabinet of the corner unit in the large kitchen and eyed the small selection. He pulled out a bottle of whisky, checked he was alone, and took a quick couple of swigs. Deliberately, he put the bottle away, stowing the key back to its safe home.

It was just enough to fortify him as Mo never wanted to see the return of the drunk father he'd become immediately after Catarina's passing. Glancing at the clock, he realised he needed to wake the sleeping duo. Ben wouldn't sleep later if he let him nap much longer. Mo strolled back to the sitting room. Poor Shereen, Ben had probably exhausted her. Mo's mum was used to Ben's brand of energy levels, but it had taken her a while.

I should have warned Shereen.

Taking a moment, Mo leaned against the doorframe and watched his friend sleep, something he hadn't done since they were both sixteen. With her freckles still standing out on her golden-caramel skin and her long hair tied back into a soft ponytail, she looked younger than her thirty-two years. If she opened her eyes, he would see the same hazel with brown flecks encircling her irises. He smiled at the platforms beside the large sofa. She still loved to pair the wedges with casual jeans and t-shirts. A bracelet hung on her left wrist. Not the one he'd given her years ago, this one had more charms—a pandora, he thought.

In so many ways, she was still the same Shereen he'd spent so much time with from the age of two, when he'd arrived in England and his family moved into the house next door, until his sixteenth year. How anyone could be playful and shy at the same time, he didn't know, but Shereen was that. Strong yet vulnerable. Not exactly a leader, but someone people turned to for advice—a friend who would commiserate with you. Despite him always helping her when she was very young, she was always his peace.

They'd spent so many years apart now that he wasn't as sure about her as he used to be. From the moment Shereen went to Leeds University at eighteen, they never spent as much time together. Life had taken over, which he supposed was a usual occurrence. They were both busy, or her parents visited her instead of Shereen coming here so Mo could see her too. Though they'd caught up with phone calls and FaceTime, it wasn't the same as their childhood and early teen years. There were things he didn't know about her now, like when she got her right ear pierced a second time.

However, what hadn't changed was the feeling of peace that enveloped him when he was with her. He realised now that he'd worried too much about telling Shereen his idea of spending more time together. What was more natural for such long-time friends than that? How many times had Tae Joon called him up to have a drink? Mo had done the same thing with Tae Joon, with Noah and Eli, or Brad.

Mo wouldn't have let Shereen go back to Leeds without spending some time with her and catching up. He considered, that there were so many things they enjoyed doing together, and an idea crept into his mind that would delight her and spark her competitive spirit in equal measure.

"Hi. I can't believe I dosed off," Shereen blinked, sleepy eyes widening.

"I can. When we were younger, you were always falling asleep."

Shereen shook her head. "You seem to be remembering inaccurately again. I'm going to wash my face." She stood up and left the sitting room.

Mo frowned. Was that embarrassment? Had her cheeks gone a little pink? He'd seen her sleeping lots of times, and she'd never been embarrassed. He shrugged. It must be his imagination. Ben had slid down the sofa as Shereen extricated herself but slept on. Mo considered waking him but instead scooped the little boy up and out to the car, strapping him in and heading back into the house for his things.

"Here." In the hallway, Shereen handed him Ben's backpack and his own bag.

"Thanks for taking care of him."

"Since when did we need thanks between us? Stop being cheesy."

Mo laughed. "I've missed you."

"You're too busy to have missed me."

Mo walked to the door, Shereen following behind. He looked at Ben sleeping in the back seat of his car. Then he turned to Shereen. "As it's Saturday tomorrow, are you free in the afternoon?"

Shereen walked outside with him. Even though it was early July and the weather should have been hot and cloying, there was a slight breeze in the air.

"I'm taking my mum shopping in the morning, but I'll be free from about three. I won't make your football game, though."

Most Saturday mornings, Mo and Ben picked up Dad and headed to the local park to play football in the Angolan team organised by Big Nelo, a fellow Angolan. If his brother-in-law couldn't make it, he also picked up Sara's twins, Jay and Raquel. Noah and Eli usually met them there.

"You still don't like playing football?" She'd hated it at school.

"You know me. I don't mind watching it, though. But I prefer to spend my Saturday mornings doing more fun things."

"Want to go biking in the afternoon?"

"I haven't been biking since I left. So I don't even know if my bike is okay. I'll get it checked tomorrow afternoon, and if it's okay, I'd love to. But Sunday would work better."

"See you Sunday afternoon then," Mo confirmed.

Mo decided to forgo Ben's regular bath time when he arrived home and put him straight to bed. After changing into a pair of soft pants and a t-shirt, he pulled his wedding album from under the coffee table and gazed at the photos of Catarina. Occasionally, his mind wandered to Shereen standing in front of his parent's house, and excitement filled him at the thought of their biking trip on Sunday.

***

Shereen lay in bed wearing her favourite pyjamas, unable to sleep. After her exciting day with Ben, she was exhausted and had expected oblivion when her head hit the pillow. Instead, the stars she'd installed on the ceiling when she was fourteen glimmered in the darkness.

She turned on her side and tried to pinpoint what was bothering her. Maybe the nap she had was keeping her awake? She sighed, taking Ben to and from school, then the afternoon at the park had been lovely. She'd always loved children and wanted a bunch of her own but had never spent time with one by herself for any longer than a couple of hours. Sophie's baby was too small, and the new mama couldn't bear to part with her little girl for longer.

If Shereen couldn't wait to get a family of her own, why had she refused Liam's proposal? She could be planning her wedding and at least be trying for a baby by now. No one bothered about a pregnant bride these days. Plenty of women had children at thirty-two, but she wasn't young anymore in making baby terms. Since she wanted at least four, she'd always planned to start having children when she was young. Liam had wanted kids too.

What had happened in the sitting room with Mo? Why did she get embarrassed when he'd caught her sleeping? Why worry about sleep in her eyes and run off to check? Had her heart jumped when Mo mentioned the picnic? She was over Mo, got over him a long time ago, and hadn't thought about him romantically for years.

Shereen just got a little more comfortable when her phone rang, making her jump. Who was calling her at ten at night? Picking it up from the bedside table where it was charging, she squinted at the caller ID, frowning at the name.

"Are you okay?" she asked tentatively.

"Still worried about me?"

"Yes, Liam, when you call at ten pm."

"You never used to mind, even when I called later." His voice was soft, a caress. "It's Friday night anyway."

Shereen sat up on the bed cross-legged, her back against the wall. That was true, and she didn't really mind. She just didn't want to encourage him, only to hurt him again. "Liam, if you keep calling, it's going to be hard for you to find someone else. You should be out there finding the woman of your dreams.

"You're the woman of my dreams."

Shereen wished she could be happy with that. Didn't every woman want to hear those words? Liam was very handsome, like a world-class model. His blue eyes and eclectic mix of Slavic, Irish, Caribbean and Hispanic genetics, paired with his impressive height, made him a gift any woman would love to have for at least a few hours. When paired with his wonderful personality and the millions in his bank account, not to mention the billions in his family's coffers, he turned into a man a woman could love for the rest of her life. Any sane woman, at least. Ergo, Shereen was not sane.

In the short time they'd dated, Shereen almost convinced herself he could be the one. She'd imagined saying yes if he proposed, believing she'd found someone to spend the rest of her life with. But when Liam got down on one knee to propose, she'd frozen, the *yes* she'd practised, that could have made her a mum, stuck in her throat.

Was it because they'd only dated for a year? That was the explanation she'd given Liam. She wasn't ready, and if he could wait, she'd be able to say yes at some point. Only she didn't know when that would be, and because he was such a wonderful man, she hadn't wanted to make him wait when she wasn't sure. Even then, she'd known that if she said yes, it'd be because she didn't want to upset him, and that wasn't the right basis for marriage. So she'd worked up the courage to say she couldn't marry him, breaking his heart and their relationship.

Since then, she'd begun a soul-searching mission to find out why she'd been unable to commit to not one but two incredible men, and she still hadn't found the answer.

"How is business?" Shereen asked, shaking those melancholy thoughts away.

"Not bad. But how is your mum?"

The answer was so like him. Liam rarely talked about the things bothering him. No matter how much she'd tried, she'd never been able to get him to talk about his demons. Nor did he open up about the difficulties he faced running his chain of pubs and dealing with his family's multibillion shipping empire. Could that be another reason why she hadn't accepted his proposal?

Shereen paused before answering, wanting to think about Liam's question. "Physically, she's recovering fast, but I think this fall has given her a shock."

"I wish I was there with you."

"Liam—"

A laugh down the line. "As a friend. If Kate or Heena had said that, you wouldn't be bothered."

Shereen's lips curved up. "I didn't date them."

"You go on dates with them, and Sophie and Andrea, all the time.

Shereen thought about her friends. She'd only been in London for a couple of weeks but already missed her daily lunch dates with at least one of them. They met at university and, apart from Andrea who'd moved to Bradford, they all settled in Leeds.

"Shereen, we agreed to be friends, remember?"

How could she forget? They'd only broken up recently, so they were getting used to their new relationship status. "Sorry, Liam," Shereen said, always on edge whenever they talked about their relationship. She was confused about why she couldn't settle down and why no one ever seemed to be the right person for her to marry.

They chatted until Shereen's eyes began to close.

Saturday Shereen was busy with washing her mum's hair before their late morning shopping trip that turned into lunch. Then she took her bike to Halfords in the afternoon before a relaxing evening watching a movie and eating popcorn with her parents.

The sky was grey with clouds threatening to release a colossal downpour when she woke up early Sunday morning, but by lunchtime, the weather had changed its mind, and the sun was shining. So when Mo arrived at her house, Shereen was ready, with her bike, a picnic basket and blanket waiting in the hallway.

"Have fun," Mum called from the couch as Shereen wheeled the bike out.

Dad greeted Mo and Ben, then stood on the doorstep, watching Mo load Shereen's bike on the car. He waved before turning back indoors.

"Auntie Shereen, look," Ben pointed to the side of his mouth. "I lost another tooth."

Shereen looked back at Ben strapped into his car seat. She smiled at the delight on his face. “Did you put it under your pillow?”

“I did. Dad said, the tooth fairy will bring me a big gold coin.”

Shereen looked at Mo. “Did he?” She stopped herself from smiling at the image of Mo wearing a fairy’s costume.

Mo glared at her, but his expression made her want to laugh harder.

Ben nodded. “Last time, I got a gold coin too. Dad got me a coin jar to put all my coins in.”

“What do you want to buy?”

Ben cocked his head; the way Mo sometimes did. Shereen blinked in surprise.

“A horse.”

“A horse?” Shereen looked at Mo, who nodded and shrugged. “Do you mean a toy horse?” Shereen asked.

“No, a real one.” Ben frowned. “Maybe a pony? A pony wouldn’t be too big for me to ride. I wouldn’t be scared to ride a pony. When I’m bigger, I can ride a proper horse.”

“You’re going to learn to ride a horse?”

Ben’s big eyes shone. He nodded.

“I didn’t know you loved horses that much,” Shereen said.

Mo eased the car onto the motorway towards Leman Park. "It's his new love. We watched Beauty last night, and Ben fell in love with a horse."

"Ew, Daddy. I'm not in love with a horse. I want to ride horses. That's different."

Shereen saw Mo's smile and couldn't resist the tug on her lips.

"Auntie Shereen, have you watched Beauty?"

The rest of the way to the park, Ben wanted to know everything Shereen remembered about Beauty.

After parking the car, Mo and Shereen unloaded their bikes. Shereen took a deep breath in, smelling the freshness in the air, anticipating the ride to come. She loved biking but hadn't done it for a long time. She looked around, away from the car park to the massive spread of green trees and grass all around them.

Mo strapped Ben in the seat at the back of his bike and put his helmet on. He looked at Shereen, his lips tugging up.

"Ready?"

Shereen took off, riding slowly in the car park, testing her muscles, ready for the challenge.

Mo rode up alongside her, keeping pace. As they left the car park and joined a cycling path, they sped up.

At first, Shereen thought only of the thrill riding in such a large, open space. Whizzing past lakes, grassy areas, plant and flower beds, she gloried in the beauty of nature. She gazed at Mo and Ben a couple of times, happiness filling her when she saw that same joy reflected in their gazes. Most of the time, however, she switched off her brain and marvelled at how her body remembered the feel of the bike.

Once the initial euphoria abated, she realised she'd automatically taken the path she and Mo had ridden sixteen years ago, the last summer they'd come to the park. Not easily accessible by bus or train, they'd only visited three times during school holidays. The last one she recalled was a blazing hot August day. Her passion was 'Take That', and her favourite in the group, Robbie Williams, adorned the t-shirt she wore. She still remembered Mo's teasing.

Shereen slowed as she passed a large, beautiful pond. It was still the same, with the weeping willow on the left side, the ducks swimming along, and the small, arched footbridge across the narrower end. The wide footpaths and beautiful picnic areas were familiar too, but some things were new. Like the young tree a few metres down the path and the bench on the east side of the park, dedicated to someone who had done a lot for the area.

Mo had slowed down and was gazing at the

tree too. Finally, he stopped, and Shereen pulled up beside him.

"They planted that a couple of years ago."

"It looks like a maple tree." It had a light grey, smooth bark, and the leaves were palmate and lobed.

"Auntie Shereen, how did you know that?"

Shereen laughed. "I love trees."

"Daddy loves trees too."

Mo removed Ben's helmet and ruffled his hair. "It was Auntie Shereen that got me loving trees." Mo replaced the headgear, adjusting the straps again.

"Really?" Ben looked at Shereen.

"Well," Shereen said, sitting back on her bike, "All I did was tell your daddy a story about a tree in my back garden, and I had him hooked. That just shows he always loved trees; he just didn't know about it."

"So, is it the same with horses and me?"

Shereen's eyebrows lifted. She looked at the pained look on Mo's face, a wicked feeling coming over her. She wasn't going to rescue him. Besides, it looked like Ben's personality was very much like his father's. Kind of possessive, a little clingy, the type that once they liked something, it was for life.

"Kind of."

"See, Daddy. If you buy me a pony, I'll ride it every day. Promise I won't get tired of it."

"I'm thinking about it, remember?" Mo turned to Shereen. "Thanks a lot," he mouthed. Then, when Shereen smiled, he glared at her. "Let's have lunch."

Mo rode off, and Shereen followed, shaking her head. As she wondered if Mo was thinking back to their last ride, he veered off the path towards a copse. Although it didn't look like it, inside the cluster of trees was an area wide enough for a family to picnic. Mo dismounted and pushed his bike round to a tiny aperture, just tall enough to get a bike through. Helping Ben down and placing the bike beside a tree, Mo crouched and disappeared into the clearing. Ben followed.

Once Ben was through, Shereen left her bike and tailed him, hoping no one was inside. Grinning like a Cheshire cat at the quiet and emptiness, she twirled, uncaring that she looked like a child.

Mo and Ben laughed, and Ben twirled alongside her, opening his arms wide.

"I feel dizzy," he said after a while. Shereen picked him up before Mo could reach him. She placed him on her shoulders, held his arms wide and carried on twirling.

"I'm going to get our lunch," Mo said, lips lifted.

Feeling a little guilty, Shereen stopped twirling and placed Ben on the ground, laughing as he staggered around before lying down to wait for the world to stop spinning. "Sorry, I can't help just now. I'll be okay in a minute," She called out to Mo as he pushed his bike through to the clearing then returned for hers. By the time he was lining it up next to his, she felt steady and went out for the picnic and blankets. Ben followed.

Shereen gave the blankets to Ben, who scampered off, while she carried the picnic basket and some bags Mo had brought. Inside, Mo and Ben each held a side of one of the blankets, stretching it out to cover the ground. That was the exact spot at which she and Mo had lunched that hot summer day. They followed with the other blanket, making a large area for them to picnic on.

"Auntie Shereen. Put the food here."

Shereen shook herself and walked towards them. They placed the food on the blanket and sat down to eat.

"Rissois," Shereen shouted, picking a golden, breaded half-moon sized pastry. She took a bite, chewed and sighed. "My favourite. I like it when Auntie Rebecca makes them with meat or tuna, but these prawn ones are the best."

Ben nodded, chewing one too.

"You've always loved them. I can't even remember how many chores you did for me in exchange for a few of these."

Shereen laughed. "Your mum must have been puzzled, wondering why you always asked her to make these when they weren't your favourite."

"It could have worked forever if Maria hadn't found out."

Shereen laughed. They'd been fourteen when Maria, Mo's eldest sister, had returned home unexpectedly and found Shereen doing the dishes Mo was supposed to wash. She'd wanted to know what was going on. Of course, if anyone else had found them out, they would have been okay. But Maria had an intrinsic ability to detect a lie, no matter how small, and she'd wrangled the sordid truth out of them.

"I always knew she'd make a wonderful lawyer." Mo was proud of Maria, who had become a human rights advocate. "I pity anyone she's facing off against."

"You're more scared of your eldest sibling than you are your Mum."

"The only time I'm scared of Mum is when she's matchmaking. Apart from that, she's the sweetest mum anyone could wish for. But my eldest sister—" Mo mock shivered before carrying on, "—is like a dog with a bone. She just won't let go. And she has an answer for everything. Arguing with her just gives me a headache."

"She's got the best persuasive skills I've ever known." Shereen recalled the couple of times she'd debated with Maria. "At first, it feels like she's agreeing with your point, but then, without you being aware, you completely believe her point of view. Yeah, I remember that feeling."

Mo and Ben reached for the last Bajan fishcake at the same time. "Ben, I didn't know you liked those. I'll make you some," Shereen said as Mo split the pastry in half. "It's one of my mum's favourite foods." Shereen's mum was addicted to the deep-fried cod fishcake wrapped in a herb-filled spicy batter she used to make. It was one of the first foods she ate whenever she visited Barbados, her Grandma's native nation.

"They are my favourite too! Thank you, Auntie Shereen!"

Ben fell asleep soon after eating. Mo scooped him up and laid him down on the blanket, a little away from where they were sitting. He fished out a capulana - a thin African cloth – and covered him.

"Will he be warm enough? It's still cool and a little dark in here." Shereen lowered her voice, afraid to wake Ben. She tried to see behind the trees to the perimeter of the clearing. The tree branches above blocked most of the sunlight, giving the clearing the feel of a large room. A bed, a sofa, and a few other items could almost make the clearing a home. "Do you think anyone else knows about this spot?"

Mo shrugged. Shereen watched the way his muscles rippled under the snug, white t-shirt he was wearing before lifting a plastic wineglass and sipping ice-cold, white wine.

Any woman's eyes would do the same, she reasoned.

She'd noticed the same thing a few times with Noah and Eli, Mo's brothers, although not as often as with Mo because their chests just weren't as awesome as their brother's.

"Ben and I come here every couple of months or so, and this place is always empty. So hopefully, no one knows about it."

Shereen giggled.

"What's so funny?"

"Picturing you fighting, arguing that this is your spot."

"I'd be tempted too." Mo smiled back at her before his gaze shifted to Ben. "He'll be fine." He packed away the picnic remains, and Shereen helped.

After they put everything away, Mo laid down with his arms behind his head.

Shereen almost groaned. That's how he'd lain when they were here before, and she wanted to forget, had thought she'd forgotten, that summer.

Almost everything Mo was doing now brought back bittersweet memories because that was a bittersweet time. A few weeks after the fateful prom, when she'd decided against telling Mo how she felt in fear of losing their friendship, she'd still been longing for him.

Recalling that time reminded her of those old feelings for Mo. They didn't feel distant right now, so Shereen laid down too, matching his pose.

"You didn't tell me you'd been coming here all this time," she said, keeping her voice neutral, knowing there were some things Mo didn't like to talk about.

It was a while before he answered. "Because I didn't."

Shereen waited, looking up at the branches trying to find where the slivers of light came from that entered their hideout.

"I didn't come here with Catarina. She didn't like biking. So I only started coming here again when Ben was about one and started toddling around in here."

Shereen hoped Mo would carry on talking about Catarina and how much he missed her. Because he never did with her. Even though she hoped he spoke of her with his family or other friends, she doubted it. Because that's what Mo was like. The most demonstrative member of the Rodrigo family, yet he just wouldn't talk about it whenever it was something to do with him. It could take him months before opening up about something that upset him, though Shereen could usually talk to him about anything in this world. Anything except Catarina.

After his wife passed, Shereen had tried to be there for Mo. She'd come down to London knowing how devastated Mo would be, but even then, she'd been shocked by the way Mo's eyes looked. It was as if something inside him had died too. Even after the funeral, she'd stayed in London, to be with his family as they tried to console him. But all Mo had wanted those first few weeks was to be left alone. That hurt because even though she'd moved on from him, she hated seeing him in so much pain and being unable to help him.

Sometimes, she'd insisted on spending time with him, and he'd let her. She'd drink with him, or they'd just sit together in silence until she fell asleep. Other times he'd tell her to go away and shut the door before she had a chance to squeeze herself inside.

"I didn't bike either. It was so much of a bother to take the bike up to Leeds, and I didn't want to buy another bike when I had one here. So this is my first time since I left home."

Mo snorted. "I could tell. You were tired before we stopped, but stubborn madam didn't want to admit it."

Shereen gasped. "Don't call me that." She lifted her head and looked over at Ben before lowering her voice. "Take it back."

Mo's chest shook. "I don't think you've ever stopped being stubborn. If the shoe fits—"

Shereen turned to glare at him. Mo turned too until they were lying on their sides, in a staring match. She'd hated being called that, because she liked to consider herself a peacemaker.

"Okay." Mo gave in and laid on his back again. "Are you still running?"

Shereen was happy he'd remembered her new passion. "It's in my blood now. I think I'm addicted to it." She went jogging every morning before sitting down to write. She started in her first year away from home to combat her homesickness and missing Mo. When she ran, especially at first, she'd struggled so much all she could think about was the pain in her legs and the struggle for breath. Then, as she improved, she started enjoying the scenery around the beautiful Leeds countryside. It had helped so much; she'd kept it up. Now, it had become a part of her daily life. "Monday to Saturday."

"Where do you go here? To the local park?"

"Why, don't you think small, local parks are beautiful enough?" She glanced at him. He'd picked a blade of grass and was folding it. "We had so much fun there."

Mo grinned. “Until we were about twelve or so. Remember how you used to love the swing?”

I remember how you never seemed to tire of pushing me. And how high I used to go.

“Eli too,” Shereen said, remembering how Mo’s youngest brother had followed them everywhere. Noah, who was the eldest brother, had stopped hanging out with them by then.

They were silent for a moment. Mo lifted her arm. “That’s a pretty bracelet. Is it new?” Shereen looked at their arms, hers a golden caramel and his a warm milk chocolate. “It was a birthday present from Sophie.” She wondered if Mo remembered the charm bracelet he’d given her on her sixteenth birthday.

Has Mo held onto my arm longer than necessary?

Just as she began turning to look at him, he let go of her again. She closed her eyes and moved back—breathing deeply and slowly.

“How is your new book going?”

For the rest of their time in the clearing, she told him about her current work in progress, explaining the story in detail. Mo was good at finding plot holes, so he had become a great sounding board over the years. Especially so, during the first year after his wife’s passing. When he’d started talking again, her work was what they talked about the most because it was a neutral topic that wouldn't cause him pain.

When Ben woke up, they biked back to the car. As they left the park, Shereen watched the greenery recede into the distance through the rear window and vowed she'd take up biking again. At first, she hadn't continued because it brought back too many memories of Mo, but that was over a long time ago. It was time.

"Glad you came today?" Mo asked as she turned back to face the front of the car.

"Yes. I've decided to take up biking again."

"I felt the same the first time I came back."

Shereen took in his profile as he concentrated on the road ahead.

"Shall we come back in a couple of weeks? There's so much of the park you haven't seen. Even Ben and I haven't seen everything." Mo glanced at her.

Shereen agreed. She was looking forward to it already.

Chapter 5

Mo tucked Ben in, surprised his son hadn't fallen asleep during his bedtime story.

"Daddy," Ben said, a curious expression on his face. Mo recognised that look and wondered what had sparked Ben's interest.

"Today was the best day ever." He sat up and threw his arms around Mo. Surprised, Mo hugged him back.

"Did you enjoy biking with Auntie Shereen? Was it more fun than just us guys?"

Ben giggled. Mo tickled him until Ben squealed for him to stop. Breathless, Ben laid back on his bed.

"Silly Daddy," he said, eyes sleepy. "It was best because I saw Mummy at the cemetery AND Auntie Shereen at the park."

When Ben's eyes closed, Mo switched off the light, headed to the kitchen and grabbed a beer. He agreed with his son wholeheartedly. Today, he had felt more alive and hopeful than he had for a long time.

He loved biking with his son but having Shereen share the experience had given Mo some of the joy he had been craving. Shereen loved biking the same way he did, would look at nature for hours without the need for conversation. There was no need to talk when, just seeing her smile of enjoyment, had given him a buzz.

It had been the perfect plan to spend more time with Shereen. They were friends and could enjoy each other's company without worrying that things might get complicated.

The day had been a salve to Mo's soul, and he couldn't prevent a huge smile from spreading ear to ear as he moved to the sitting room to switch on the DVD player. But before he pressed play, he recalled the day Catarina told him she was pregnant nearly five years ago.

Mo exited Hackney Central Station, eyes scanning the crowd for Catarina. He spotted her a few steps away from the main thoroughfare, standing proudly in her three-inch heels and the golden, crochet hook sun dress she loved. Although she didn't quite reach five feet six, he'd always been able to pick her out in a crowd. For him, she stood apart from everyone else. Now he'd found her, Mo slowed, but she lifted her head and looked directly at him.

Eyes glued to hers, Mo drank her in as he approached before finally being close enough to wrap her in his arms and kiss her lips. She was just too beautiful from head to toe—her hair the same mass of curls as when they met at the age of sixteen that framed her heart-shaped face and reached just past her shoulders; her large liquid brown eyes still mesmerised him; to him, her pert nose was the most perfect in the world.

Laughing, she linked their arms and started walking towards the location of the best Indian restaurant in Hackney. "We'll never be able to visit one of those countries where kissing or hugging in public is forbidden, you know."

Mo laughed too. "Why not? We'll just spend all our time in our bedroom." Mo adjusted the strap of his bag. "It's rare for you to be this early. Were you too excited to wait to celebrate?"

"Year four, cardiothoracic trainee surgeon Dr Rodrigo was born ready to celebrate."

Mo shook his head. "My wife has no modesty."

"Your wife worked her arse off to be ahead in her training and passed her exams with flying colours. Why should she be modest? Wouldn't that be considered coy?"

"You and Tae Joon are so alike. At least you look cute when you brag." Mo steered Catarina around a large group of people. Though it was seven o'clock, the early June evening sun was still shining, and the street was packed with folks not yet ready to go home.

“He’s the one that likes to compete.” Catarina tightened her hold on Mo when someone brushed too close to her. “We’re neck and neck at the moment, but we’ll see what the future holds.”

“You mean you’re going to do your best to become a consultant before him even if it kills you? Never mind your poor husband who’s lonely when you’re working nonstop.”

“Oh please, Dr Rodrigo. You’re just as bad as I am. Lonely my arse. You’re either conducting research or writing up your experiments, and if not, you’ve got your nose inside a medical journal.”

“Sometimes, I wonder if we’ll be the type of parents who fight over who’s going to feed the baby.”

Catarina snorted. Mo opened the door of the restaurant and let her enter.

“I know you’re going to be a wonderful dad. It’s one of the reasons I married you.” She looked around the restaurant as they waited to be seated.

“Not because of my great looks and six-pack?”

Catarina’s gaze slid to Mo’s abdomen. “That too.”

As they followed the waiter towards a table at the back of the restaurant, Mo took in the vibrant colours of the walls and tablecloths, the food's tantalising aromas, and neatly organised tables. Spicy food wasn't his favourite, but he'd wanted to try this place for the last three years. Marrying two years ago and buying a house a year later had meant they couldn't afford it before now, but Mo wanted to spare no expense to celebrate Catarina's achievements. Though the waiting list was three months long, Tae Joon knew the owner and had helped him book a table.

"I can't believe I'm actually here," Catarina said after the waiter left. "I'm going to eat until I burst." She opened the menu and perused the variety of dishes.

Mo groaned, hoping she wouldn't over order then ask for a doggy bag to take the rest home. That was a pet peeve that even Catarina could not make him overcome. He flicked through the menu, looking for the least spicy foods he could find.

The waiter returned to take their food and drinks order, and as he left, a lively song started playing.

"Should we go clubbing tonight? We haven't been in ages," Catarina suggested, ignoring Mo's raised eyebrows over her order of a mocktail.

"As far as I know, you're working tomorrow. If we'd waited until next week to celebrate when you have the whole weekend off, we could have managed it." Unfortunately, Tae Joon's friend could only squeeze them in on a weekday as the restaurant was way too busy on weekends. It was a huge favour he'd managed to fit them in on a Friday.

Their drinks arrived—Mo's a frothy golden beer, while Catarina's was a myriad of colours reflecting off shaved ice. She sipped her drink with a purr of appreciation. "Querido! Just because we've been working hard and saving the last few years doesn't mean we should forget we're twenty-eight. Besides, next week is too far away. And I'm only on call. So if I'm lucky, I won't even need to go in and will just get a few phone calls."

"Risky." Mo knew his wife well. Maybe she really wanted to go clubbing, but she'd never do it when she had to work the following day, even if it was only an on-call shift. She was too much of a perfectionist for that.

"Let's go next Saturday. I don't know what's got over me. I want to go partying. Sometimes I miss our first couple of years at uni. We thought we had so much studying to do, but we always found some time to party."

"Mum thought you were going to ruin me."

They laughed together at the thought.

"Mama Rebecca took her time warming up to me. She had me worried. I think she only fully accepted me when we got engaged."

Mo shook his head. "She was just a little sad you got your paws on me so young. I was only seventeen when I told her I was going to marry you."

Catarina wiped her eyes.

"What's the matter?" Mo asked. The last couple of weeks, Catarina had seemed more emotional, crying during a movie, shouting at him for leaving a dish in the sink, and a few other overreactions entirely out of character for her. Surprised, Mo had put it down to the stress of her work and training, but here she was crying again at a nostalgic memory when she should be enjoying their celebration.

"I know I've been a little moody lately. This afternoon, I realised my period was late and did a pregnancy test."

Catarina stopped talking as two waiters approached with trays full of plates and bowls. Mo stared at her, his heart beating faster while he waited for them to transfer it to their table and leave.

"And?"

"I'm pregnant." She gave him a slight smile waiting for his response.

Joy spread through Mo, and he couldn't stop the shout of triumph leaving his lips. About to get out of his seat and hug his wife, he remembered her work. "I'm over the moon, but we planned on waiting until you'd finished your specialisation."

Catarina laughed. "God had other plans. Besides, who am I?"

Mo laughed too, shaking his head. "One of the smartest, hard-working women in the world."

"That's right. I'm already miles ahead in my training. So it won't take me long to catch up. Besides, I'm doing the carrying, and you can do most of the staying up late once our baby comes along."

"Let's take some time to think about this," he reasoned, not wanting to rush her over such an important decision.

"Mo, it's our baby. I want to keep it, and I know you want that too."

Mo swallowed, happiness and concern filling him in equal measure. Happiness won. He stood and rounded the table to lift Catarina, giving her a twirl.

"They're going to ask us to leave in a minute," Catarina warned into his ear.

Mo helped her back to her seat before he looked around. Curious glances were directed at him.

"My wife just told me she's pregnant," he said to the people sitting the closest and nodded when their curiosity turned into smiles and congratulations.

"Come on, let's eat. I'm ravenous." Catarina said when he sat down. She tucked into her spicy beef dish, sighing in delight.

Her pregnancy had been a breeze. Catarina remained healthy and happy, if emotional, without any problems. She'd even stopped working at thirty-nine weeks, although she carried on reading medical journals and doing research.

Chapter 6

It was hard to get out of bed the next morning. Shereen groaned as she forced herself to get up, knowing that if she didn't stretch or jog, her muscles would stiffen more throughout the day. So she stretched on her bedroom floor, dressed in her favourite leggings, sports bra and a baggy tee, and left the house. She ran around the block, surprised anew by the changes in her childhood neighbourhood. She finished her light jog with a lap around the park. It was so beautiful she decided to take Ben there that afternoon.

After two weeks of taking care of her mum and only checking emails, Shereen was inspired by discussing her book with Mo at the picnic and decided to return to her work. She took a revitalising shower before the smell of her dad cooking breakfast lured her to the kitchen.

"You're spoiling me with all this food, Dad," she said, greeting him with a kiss to the cheek. "At this rate, I won't want to go back to Leeds, and you'll find yourself lumbered with a grown-up daughter who refuses to leave."

Her dad served her sausages, egg and bacon on a plate. "I wouldn't mind that. I miss you, and I think your mum does too." He placed the plate in front of her.

When did Mum and Dad have time to worry about her? She picked her knife and fork, watching her father's movements. Over the years, they'd sometimes said they missed her, during phone conversations or when they visited. But now, there seemed a seriousness to her dad's words.

"I'll visit more. Besides, it's much easier for me to come down than both of you going up," Shereen said, watching his reaction.

"That would be nice. Are you set on staying there permanently?"

Shereen forked a bite of eggs and chewed slowly. Was she? She loved her life in Leeds. Up at seven, she jogged before breakfast and worked until lunchtime. Most days, she'd meet up with at least one of her friends for lunch and then work in the afternoon. Her evenings consisted of reading or Netflix, but sometimes she'd go out with friends or on a date. She did miss her parents, but she talked to them every day, so it almost felt as if she lived near them.

Shereen's plan had always been to move closer to them in twenty or so years, but looking at her father, she realised how much older he seemed.

She'd noticed the grey hair, but now his eyes seemed old too. When he walked back to the cooker, his back was straight, but his steps were slower. She gulped. "That depends on what you and Mum decide. At the moment, I'm happy living there. You know how beautiful it is." The trouble was she knew how much her parents loved London. "Later on, I want to live close to you. If I can't convince you to come up, I might move back."

"Your mum would like that—to see more of you." He washed his hands. "I'm going up to get her now."

"Shout if you need help." Shereen washed up and looked at the clock. The doorbell rang.

"Okay?" Mo asked as he ushered Ben in.

"Just a little tired." Shereen eyed the blue shirt Mo was wearing, fascinated by how it contoured his broad shoulders. She dragged her gaze away and placed a hand on top of Ben's head, trying to ground herself. "Have a good day," she and Ben called and waved, closing the door after Mo had set off to the station.

After running Ben to school when it was time, Shereen went straight to her bedroom, opened her current work in progress and checked where she was in the story. Switching on her laptop, she turned up the volume on her playlist, set the timer to fifty-five minutes and started writing. The best part of her job was writing the first draft of a book.

She planned her stories out, chapter by chapter, scene by scene, so she knew where she wanted to go with the story when it was time to write. But in each scene, she let herself go and sometimes she had to adjust her plan because the story had taken her somewhere she hadn't envisaged, or she'd come up with another idea as her fingers tapped wildly. Part of the pleasure was the sensory of the typing itself. She often joked with her friends that she could make a living as a typist if her books stopped selling.

Just before twelve, Shereen picked up Ben and after lunch with her mum and dad, she took him next door for a nap.

"I'm not sleepy, Auntie Shereen. See, my eyes are wide open." Ben widened his eyes.

"How about I tell you a story. It might help you sleep." It was so hard resisting the plea in Ben's liquid eyes. She'd talked to Ben a few times over the phone and had always thought he was cool. The couple of times she'd held him as a baby had endeared him to her. But these past few days, she'd fallen in love with him to the point where she would give him everything he wanted. And that was going to put her in Mo and Rebecca's bad books. Ben's pleading eyes and sweet voice disabused her idea that she'd be a disciplined mum.

Ben nodded.

"Does Nana have any story books?"

"She's read all those to me." Ben scratched his head. "Daddy said your job is to write stories. Will you write one for me? I have a lot of gold coins."

Shereen smiled. "I'll make you a story for free, okay?"

Her heart melted when his wide smile brought out that sweet dimple, and she thought about what kind of story he might like—horses, of course.

"High up in the clouds, in the land of Cavalo Terra, there were many magnificent horses. But the bravest and strongest of all were horse brothers Leonardo and Romeo..." she carried on making up the story, modulating her voice, using her hands and body to help bring it alive.

She'd been narrating for about ten minutes when Ben's eyelids began to close, amused as he repeatedly tried to open them again. When he finally lost the battle, Shereen's eyes strayed to the photo on the bedside table of the whole Rodrigo family. Taken only a year after Rebecca gave birth to Eli, it showed a three-year-old Mo and the then very young Rodrigo children. Shereen had always liked the picture, and she'd been glad to see it last Friday when she brought Ben up to sleep.

The whole room had made her think of the past; apart from the new bedding, it remained the same. The double bunk bed where Noah, Mo and Eli slept was still there, and the wooden wardrobes

Uncle Zacchaeus had refurbished were there too. So, even though the boys used the two new rooms in the attic whenever they slept over, the grandchildren used their old space.

She'd played in this room with Mo and the boys, but whenever she had to sleep over, she'd stayed in the girls' room across the landing. Shereen took her phone out of her pocket and took a picture of the frame, then she stood up and went downstairs.

On the kitchen table, she opened her laptop and notebook and carried on writing. When Ben woke up, she took him to the park.

"Auntie Shereen, when will you finish Leonardo and Romeo's story?"

"You want to hear the ending?"

"Can you tell me now?"

Shereen looked at the cars passing by. "It's a little noisy. I can tell you before you go to sleep tomorrow."

"You could tell me a story every time I nap," he suggested.

Shereen wished she could. Mo's parents were returning on Thursday. From Friday, she wouldn't be taking care of Ben anymore.

"I'll race you to the swings." She ran off, laughing at Ben's shout and let him catch up to her, but only a little bit.

"I won. And you started first."

"It's my shoes. They made me slow." She pointed to her high-heeled platform brown sandals."

Ben looked down too. "Trainers would make you run faster, but I'd still beat you."

They spent a couple of hours at the park, had ice cream and went home.

"Auntie Shereen, can I please help make dinner today?"

Shereen nodded, wondering what Ben could help with and not get hurt. She gave him vegetables to wash and the table to set.

"Auntie Shereen, what would you like to watch?" Ben asked when they had cleared the dinner dishes after.

She switched on the television and put Paw Patrol on.

"You like Paw Patrol too?" Ben asked.

"Yep." She'd watched it for the first time with Ben last week and, surprisingly, had enjoyed the show. They cuddled up on the sofa.

After hearing the front door open, Shereen waited for Mo to come in and waved when he popped his head in the room.

"You're awake today."

"I'm stronger than I look. How was your day?"

"Hi, Daddy!"

Mo sat on the sofa to the other side of Ben and kissed his cheek. "So busy. What did you two do this afternoon?"

"We went to the park. Would you like a drink?"

"I'll drink water. It's sweltering today."

Shereen followed him to the kitchen and greedily watched his Adam's apple bobbing up and down as he drank the cool water. What was the matter with her? Wasn't she past these kinds of thoughts regarding Mo?

Ben came into the kitchen carrying his backpack. "Auntie Shereen made a story for me. And she gave it to me for free."

"Oh?" Mo looked amused.

"It's about two horses, Leonardo and Romeo. Leonardo is so mean, Daddy, but Romeo is nice. Auntie Shereen's going to finish the story tomorrow."

Mo gave Shereen a dirty look. Shereen just laughed, happy Ben recalled so much of the story. She walked outside with Mo and Ben.

"Why did you make up a story about horses. You know I'm trying to make Ben forget about them," Mo said after he'd strapped Ben into his car seat.

"Why don't you want Ben to get into horses? It

looks to me like he's fallen in love with them."

"He wants a horse of his own. That's a bit too much, especially when he's so young. I've promised him riding lessons when he turns five, but frankly, I'm hoping it's just a phase."

***

At the end of the week, Shereen left her house at the same time Mo stepped out of his mum's. She waited for him to come round to her gate. Yesterday evening, the last day she'd looked after Ben, Eli had turned up while Shereen was seeing Mo off and suggested they all go out for a drink together.

"Where's Eli?" She asked, looking towards next door.

"He's helping out a friend tonight and can't make it. So we're on our own."

Shereen shrugged and turned towards the pub. It was no big deal Eli not coming out with them as planned. In the past, they'd arranged outings together, and occasionally Eli had pulled out at the last minute. She and Mo had always gone ahead anyway.

"Is Ben sleeping over with your mum on his own then?" Shereen asked.

Mo smiled. "The twins were happy to have a sleepover too." His sister Sara's six-year-old twins loved sleeping over at their grandmother's just as much as Ben did, especially when they were all together.

It took only ten minutes to reach the pub, and being Saturday night, it was heaving, but they managed to find a small table.

"White wine?" Mo asked.

"You know it." She watched him as he walked away. Mo was wearing faded blue jeans with a lavender t-shirt and black waistcoat, which showed how much healthier he'd become over the last year. Mo looked good in anything, but he looked particularly good in jeans. A few women checked out his bum as he walked past them and something inside Shereen lifted its ugly head. Startled, she let out a little laugh and brought her eyes to the sport on the big screen.

Just because she was his friend didn't mean she was blind. Mo had always been a good-looking man who women found attractive. She was no different. When Shereen got over Mo all those years ago, she had made a promise to herself that she, as Mo's childhood best friend, would keep it that way.

"Here." Mo placed a large wine glass in front of her, sitting down with his own San Miguel. "I bet you're glad to have more time to yourself again. Ben can be a little tiring."

Shereen looked at Mo. There was no inflection on his voice, and his face was neutral too. "I enjoyed spending time with him." And she had, a little too much for comfort. She'd missed him already and had gone next door on the pretext of seeing how Rebecca and Zacchaeus were faring after their long drive back. She'd played with Ben while Rebecca made dinner and even offered to take him if Rebecca or Zacchaeus were busy.

"He's in love with you, you know, and horses, of course. He doesn't stop talking about your stories and is giving me storytelling tips. Apparently, I need to make gestures and improve on my voices."

Shereen laughed. Mo had a lovely voice, but he'd never found pretending that much fun. Even when he was young, he'd preferred non-fiction. Her fascination with Ben must be her body's way of telling her she was ready for children. She wanted to have a little child to hold and tell stories to. To walk hand in hand with, the way Ben did, placing so much trust in her. That unconditional love was irresistible. It was calling to her.

"You've done such a good job with him, Mo."

Mo swallowed some of his beer, his Adam's apple moving. Shereen's eyes arrowed there as they had the other night at his mum's. She'd always been fascinated by Mo's Adam's apple, it was slightly more prominent than average, but instead of making him look unattractive, it did the opposite.

"I'm trying to be a good dad."

He wasn't just trying, Shereen thought. He was

doing it. Just like she always thought he would. "He's happy. You're lucky to have so much family around you. I think it's given him a sense of belonging." Shereen wanted to ask if Ben missed his mum, if he asked for her. But she didn't want to upset Mo, to see the smile leave his face.

"He's grown up so much since he started school nursery. He's more inquisitive too."

"That's good. Isn't it?"

Across the room, someone dropped something made of glass. There were claps before the pub settled down to background chatter, and they could hear themselves speak again.

"It is. But he's starting to ask more questions about Catarina."

Shereen sipped her wine as she thought about what to say. "How does that make you feel?" Her finger traced the curve of the wine glass. She made sure she was breathing slowly, encouraging herself to be calm.

Mo drank. Looked at his nearly empty glass. "I don't know," he finally answered. He swallowed the rest of the beer and stood up. "I'll get another round."

He walked off before Shereen could tell him it was her turn to buy. She sighed. He was so stubborn. She knew everyone grieved differently, but she couldn't' help thinking if Mo talked more about Catarina, he'd benefit from it. She finished her wine.

"How's Liam?" Mo asked when he returned.

Did she want to talk about her own life when Mo wouldn't talk about his? Shereen sipped at the new wine Mo had brought with him. For a moment, she thought about not answering. Maybe she could shrug her shoulders or just look into her glass.

"He's not mistreating you, is he?" Mo's eyes showed concern.

Knock it off, Shereen. Just because they were friends didn't mean they had to talk about everything. They were no longer the children who shared every aspect of their lives all those years ago. Even her girlfriends didn't discuss everything. It was her choice to tell Mo about her life and what to leave out, just like he was doing with her. If Mo needed more time, so be it. The fact that he seemed to want to stay in love with Catarina for the rest of his life shouldn't bother her that much. As a friend, worrying he might be missing out on a life companion and Ben missing out on having a mother should be all that concerned her.

But Shereen didn't want to tell him she'd broken up with Liam. She didn't want Mo to think her a failure, or worse, pity her having two failed relationships in her past. That she felt that way was bad enough.

"He's all right. And he treats me very well, thank you," Shereen lied.

"Is he the one? Are you going to get married?"

Shereen stood up. It was her turn to avoid a difficult question. "I'll get the next round." She took off, platforms tapping the floor loudly, then dawdled at the bar, letting people get in front of her.

"There you go, sweetheart." A man with tattoos all over his body pushed her in front of the bartender. Startled, Shereen mumbled her thanks and ordered. She meandered back to the table.

"You're upset," were the words Mo greeted her with.

Shereen sat down. "I'm not upset. You don't want to talk, and neither do I. I don't want to burden you with my private life when you won't do the same."

Mo's eyebrows lifted. "Ouch, that hurt."

Shereen sighed. "Sorry."

"You've changed."

She hadn't. Not really. She still hated to upset the status quo. She just didn't know what had come over her. This Shereen was not the usual Shereen.

"I like it," Mo said. "And I don't know how I feel about Ben asking more questions about Catarina. It's a good thing, but for some reason, it's also worrying."

"What kind of questions is he asking?

"Doesn't she miss him? Will she come and visit him? Do children only get one mum?"

"Ha."

"Yes, ha. Some questions are easier to answer than others."

Ben had told Shereen that Mo still took him to visit his mum's grave on Saturdays and Sundays. The way Ben talked about his mum being in heaven, she was sure Mo had explained the situation in religious, Christian terms, but it must be hard for the little boy to understand fully.

"I suppose they are normal questions. Other children probably ask him questions about his mum he can't answer yet. Remember how everyone thought my mum was my nan and would tease me about not having a mother? It's probably something similar. Is your mum still trying to get you to go on dates?"

Mo stared across the room at the big screen playing a replay football match. He thought about the daughters of his mum's friends who happened to be visiting his mum when she knew he would be there. "I hope not. I've made it clear I'm not in the market."

When Mo turned back to her, Shereen's breath

hitched. There was so much pain in his eyes, so much hurt. She wanted to make it go away, wanted to wipe away the hurt. She placed her hand on the table, moved it towards him, then stopped herself reaching for her wine glass instead. Mo's usual 'I'm all right' stare was back in place when she dared another glance. Shereen knew that look too well.

"You told her you're not ready to date?"

Mo nodded.

"I suppose, if you're not ready, it wouldn't be right for you to date just to find a mother for Ben."

"Ben has a mother."

Shereen bit her lip. "Mo, Ben knows that." She looked at him. Willed for him to understand that he'd grieved enough to start letting go. "But he's a child. Although you're doing a great job of filling in for his mum, he might want a woman who's there for him like other kids have."

Mo sighed. "I know. And for now, he has you. You can practise with Ben for when you have children. Hopefully, when he grows older, he'll find it easier to accept that his mum can't be here physically."

Four years was a long time, but Shereen knew how much Mo had loved Catarina. That kind of love wasn't easy to let go of. It's what she loved about Mo—his devotion. Once he gave his heart, it was forever. But she'd noticed a difference in him these past weeks. Was Mo enjoying life more and maybe moving towards being ready for another relationship? Or was that her wishful thinking?

Practising for her own children by playing at being Ben's Mum was fun. The problem was she was beginning to love Ben so much that she was worried she'd miss him too much when she returned to Leeds and was currently not in a position to have her own children.

"Isn't that too much to expect of Ben?"

"What should I do then?"

Open your heart to another love. Could she tell him that? Shereen shifted in her seat. "You'll have to find the answer to that," she finally said.

Mo smiled. "So, your turn. What's happening with you and Liam?"

Shereen thought about not telling him. But he'd opened up to her, and it was only fair she reciprocated. "We broke up."

Mo stared at her, his head titled to one side, his mouth opening and closing. Heat warmed her cheeks and the back of her neck. Why was she embarrassed? She hadn't done anything to be ashamed of.

"Why?" Mo's voice was even, his expression that of a friend who genuinely wanted to understand his mate.

"We weren't right for each other."

“Did you break up with him?”

“Does it matter?” Shereen scowled at him.

“It does. Did Liam do something wrong?”

Shereen took a deep breath in. “He didn’t. It just wasn’t right. I’ll know when it is.”

“He seemed like a good guy.”

“He is. We’re still friends.”

“The more I think about it, the more I believe there must have been a guy that broke your heart, and it’s making it harder for you to move on. Who was the bastard?”

Shereen’s hand tightened on the wineglass. “Wouldn’t I have told you?”

Mo shook his head. “I don’t know. I remember before you left for university, you were very reserved. Something seemed to be going on, but you wouldn’t talk about it. Remember, we had that big row.”

Shereen remembered. She’d been upset for weeks. It had taken her a long time to get over her first serious argument with Mo. At that time, she’d been debating whether to study in London or Leeds. The course at Leeds was slightly better than her favourite London university was offering, but she’d been uncertain she wanted to leave her parents, friends and yes, Mo. But that row had pushed her into choosing Leeds and the better program. She’d needed space and time to get over her crush on Mo after trying for two years and failing.

"So who was it? Was it someone at school?"

Chapter 7

"Let me get more drinks." Shereen escaped. Even if it was only for a few minutes, she needed a break. Space away from Mo's probing eyes. She went outside and stood there watching pedestrians and the Saturday evening traffic pass by. She had drunk more than she should and was getting tipsy. This one would have to be her last round.

She went back into the pub, bought their drinks and was almost at their table when someone behind her called her name. Turning, she scanned the faces in the room.

"Shereen!" Liam walked towards her a few feet from where surprise left her rooted to the spot. What was he doing here? She'd initially thought it might be Eli or an old school friend.

Liam reached for her shoulder. "Hi," he said, his blue eyes alight with amusement. The smile that charmed everyone within sight and had once upon a time made her weak at the knees.

"What are you doing here?" she blurted out. Even his charm couldn't distract her from the shock.

"I thought you'd at least be happy to see me." He mock pouted.

"Sorry, Liam. I was just so surprised. But seriously, what *are* you doing here?" Shereen admired the attractive way the shirt he was wearing enhanced his beautifully tanned arms and neck. No matter what time of the year it was, Liam always seemed to be tanned. Of course, travelling a lot to hot places helped, but Shereen thought maybe his mix of Irish, German and Indian genes helped give him an attractive tan where other men might look sunburned.

"I'm in London for business. So I thought I'd visit. You look beautiful in that red dress. It suits you."

"But how did you know I was here?" Shereen asked, too surprised to properly take in his compliment.

"I went to your house. Your dad said you were here. And before you ask why I didn't call, I did. You didn't answer."

In that case, he should have known she was busy, she thought, her eyes narrowing. Was he up to something? Before she could ask what, Mo appeared at her side.

He stretched out his hand to Liam. “Hi, I’m Mo.”

Liam shook Mo’s hand. “Liam. It’s nice to meet you finally.”

“Same here. Would you like to join us?”

“Sure,” Liam said.

Shereen helplessly watched as Mo looked around until his gaze fell on an empty chair a few tables away. As he went to get it, she glanced at Liam. He was eyeing the pub, probably taking in the busy atmosphere, the laughter, banter and décor. Liam was a brilliant entrepreneur. Once he decided on a venture, the chances of it succeeding were close to a hundred percent. He was impulsive too, one of the things she’d loved about him. Liam would drop whatever he was doing if you called and needed to hang out.

Mo came back with the chair, and they all sat down, with Liam and Mo opposite each other. Shereen looked at Mo and then to Liam as they looked each other over and wondered what Mo was thinking.

***

Mo liked the look Liam gave him. Open, honest. “What would you like to drink?” He asked.

Liam looked at the glasses Shereen had placed on the table. “Whisky on the rocks. Thanks.”

Mo nodded and left the table. It looked like Shereen and Liam needed some time to talk. As he waited for his turn to place an order, he felt an urge to look back at their table. While Liam seemed at ease, Mo knew that Shereen was uncomfortable with his sudden appearance. Given that she's just told him they'd split up, he wasn't surprised. Mo couldn't help overhearing some of their conversation; they'd talked so close to him. *What happened between those two?* Mo wondered.

Back at the table, he handed Liam the whisky and sat down. Should he leave and give these two some space? Wasn't that what he should do as Shereen's friend? Was that what she wanted? He dismissed the way his gut had constricted when Liam touched Shereen's shoulder. It was probably an unconscious feeling of protection towards his childhood best friend. It must be the same way he'd react if an unknown man had touched Maria or Sara. Shereen's greeting hadn't been amiable, and Mo had felt on edge until she'd said the man's name. He'd finish his drink and assess the situation, then leave if it looked like that was what his friend wanted. He looked across the table at Shereen. She had her eyes on her glass as if the answer to whatever she was puzzling over would be in its depths.

"This is a great place," Liam said, eyes seeming to take in every corner of the large pub.

"We're lucky to have it as our local bar. The drinks, the owners and the atmosphere are great,"

Mo said.

"I'm actually in London to look over a bar," Liam said. He explained a little more about the chain of bars he was interested in.

Mo had been in a couple of the bars Liam mentioned and chatted to him about his business. He looked at Shereen. Was she a little more relaxed? Why had she been so nervous? "Shereen has mentioned a couple of the places you worked on. She was impressed."

Liam raised his eyes in Shereen's direction.

"The Iguana," she said. "It is one of your best bars. And one of the best in the world."

Liam laughed. A free sound of appreciation, completely uninhibited. Mo noticed a few women look his way. He wondered if that was the problem. Was Liam a womaniser? Is that why Shereen had broken up with him? When a man had the looks and the billions of pounds Liam's family had, it was inevitable women and men would flock to him. Liam was solely focused upon Shereen, unaware of the attention he garnered any other quarter. That wasn't it then, as the man was clearly smitten by Shereen. Meeting Liam had only confirmed the opinion Mo had formed from what Shereen told him. Liam appeared to be the perfect partner for her.

"Everyone thinks that pub has done so well because of the great story behind it."

Shereen laughed too. "Please don't tell the story. Mo, you don't know what you'll be getting yourself into."

Shereen was laughing, that's what mattered. Besides, he was intrigued, so he encouraged Liam to carry on.

Liam spread his arms wide. "Once upon a time," his voice was deeper, more intimate.

Mo smiled. As he listened, he remembered the stories Shereen used to make up for him and Eli. Liam had the same look of deep concentration as if he truly was in the cave he was talking about, smuggling a great loot of stolen liqueur. Liam and Shereen could both command a captive audience for their storytelling. Even though Shereen must have listened to the story before, she was laughing with Mo as Liam finished his sweeping tale.

"You have a knack for storytelling," Mo said, impressed. "You should join the theatre or the cinema."

"I did consider that. But it wasn't an option at the time. I'm doing the next best thing, though, investing in the entertainment business."

Mo stood up. "It's been a few weeks since you've seen each other. I'm sure you have things to catch up on."

"You don't have to go." Shereen stood up too.

Mo looked at her. Did she need him to stay?

He no longer wanted to go. What a strange case of sibling rivalry. It had to be that, or what else could that feeling again in the pit of his stomach be? He looked again at both their faces. Liam was a good man, Shereen obviously liked him. She had to forget whoever it was that had hurt her and take a chance on being happy.

"It's okay. See you tomorrow." He stopped short of telling her to bring Liam to the barbecue at his mum's. For some reason he didn't want to do that. Anyway, Shereen knew she could invite him if she wanted to. His family would welcome Liam.

Mo waved to a couple of people he knew and left the bar, breathing in the cooler night air. He decided against taking a cab in favour of walking in an attempt to clear his head because there seemed to be some confusion in his mind. What kind of nonsense was this weird feeling?

Shereen was like a sister to him. He'd always treated her the same way he did Maria and Sara. The only difference was they were the same age. Even though Maria and Sara were older than Mo, he'd been brought up with a sense of protectiveness towards them. So it was perfectly acceptable for him to be protective of Shereen and feel that no matter how good Liam was, he'd probably never be good enough for Shereen. That was the only explanation Mo had for his feelings in the pub.

He nodded to himself as he walked along the

rows of large, terraced houses. He'd done the right thing. Just like a big brother, he'd checked out Liam then left to give Shereen time for a private chat to sort out whatever was going on between them. Liam didn't seem the type to miss an opportunity. So, if there was a chance they could sort things out, Mo was sure the man would take it up.

Mo cast his mind back to the summer he and Shereen were seventeen. It was the best summer of his life because he'd discovered he was in love with Catarina, yet also the worst as his relationship with Shereen was at its lowest.

That summer, for the first time in his life, he'd felt compelled to tell a girl he loved her. It was simultaneously one of the scariest and happiest memories of his teenage years. It hadn't even been anything special. He hadn't arranged anything—No balloons or fireworks. He'd been walking her home after a date at the cinema. His curfew was at ten, so it must have been around half past nine in the evening. Whenever he thought about that evening, he remembered the sky was clear, and the moon shone on her street as they walked along the path. But at the time, he'd just blurted it out, "Catarina Pinto, te amo."

Catarina came to an abrupt halt, and he'd been forced to stop too because he'd been holding so tightly to her hand. "Say that again," she'd told him in Portuguese."

"Te amo," he repeated. It had come out naturally, saying something absolute in his mind. But when her eyes widened, fear started to eat at him. His heart became a tight fist. What if she didn't feel the same? They'd known each other for eleven months, dated for eight, the last few months he was confident she loved him back. Wasn't she as besotted with him as he was with her? Suddenly, he wasn't sure anymore.

Time stretched—a bird flying away far into the distance, as the certainty inside him dissolved. Why was she taking so long to answer? Catarina was assertive, always knew what she wanted and didn't mind saying it. So why was she quiet?

He looked at her. The darkness masked her features so that he couldn't make out the expression in her eyes. He was still holding her hand, and he reached out for the other one.

"I love you too," she finally answered in Portuguese.

The world, a moment ago a revolving place of doubt, quieted, peaceful. Mo knew then that Catarina was the woman he wanted to marry.

But while he and Catarina grew closer, his relationship with Shereen was drifting apart. He knew he was partly to blame because dating Catarina meant he had less time to spend with Shereen.

Catarina entered their lives on their first day of sixth form. She'd come to the United Kingdom with her father – a consul of the Mozambican High Commission – and their family. As she had lived for five years in South Africa, she spoke English, but with Mo being the only Portuguese speaking student in his year group, the school asked him to show her around and help familiarise her with the year twelve timetable. Since then, they'd been inseparable. Mo was over the moon Catarina and Shereen got along so well. And that never really changed as the months and years passed. What did change was he and Shereen hung out less by themselves.

Mo had other friends and managed to juggle his time between them, and Shereen, always finding time to spend by themselves. Either they'd study together on Sunday afternoons at Shereen's house, which was quiet compared with the bedlam of Chez Rodrigo, or out, they'd go out biking which neither Eli nor any of Mo's friends seemed to enjoy.

As Mo fell for Catarina, he began spending more time alone with her. As Catarina also wanted to study medicine, it seemed perfectly normal that Catarina joined him in studying with Shereen and they moved their group to the library. But Shereen joined them less and less often, and his time at the library morphed into Catarina and Mo time.

A few months after he and Catarina started dating, he and Shereen stopped meeting by themselves and only socialised when they were with their other friends. Mo couldn't even remember why. Shereen had mentioned studying with a couple of friends who were doing the same A levels. She'd also said there was someone she liked whom she'd met at one of her mother's rallies.

He'd missed her and was sad they no longer spent so much time together, but he was pleased she'd met someone who she could be happy with in the same way he was with Catarina. She was doing well at school and still attended his family's barbecues, so he was content at seeing her every day on the walk to school and knowing she was alright. Catarina lived on the opposite side of their school, so he walked her home to hang out with her before returning home.

Mo turned the corner of his street, deep in thoughts of the past. He was bewildered when Shereen told him she was attending university so far away. Over the years, they'd chatted over the phone, Skyped, and FaceTimed. After that first time she'd said she met someone in London, she'd been more open about her dating life. Mo had shared the joys of his life with Catarina too. He and Catarina attended the party her parents threw in Leeds for her after the launch of her first book, and even though she hadn't come to London much, she'd attended his wedding.

But once more, after Catarina's death, their relationship had changed. And again, it was his fault. He'd been unable to share his grief with anyone. It was as if he'd lost the ability to speak, even to his best friend. Shereen remained close, sharing her life like before, and slowly he'd thawed out. So, the overprotectiveness he was feeling was perfectly normal. Shereen was special to him and he was just looking out for her.

Mo let himself into his house and grabbed a beer. He sat on the sofa he shared with Catarina and turned on the video of his wedding.

Even though he and Catarina had wanted to buy a flat and were aiming for a small wedding to save money, they hadn't been able to withstand their parents' will and had succumbed to the large event their mums wanted. An Angolan wedding planner approved by both mums decorated the hall, and Mo's nephews and nieces as well as Catarina's family were all conscripted into training for traditional and classical dances.

Mo watched the pageantry of the day on his screen, grateful now for the older women's intervention. How beautiful Catarina was dressed in that expensive wedding dress. Shereen looked stunning too and had attended with her boyfriend at that time, Stefano. Mo thought she'd marry him as they'd been dating for three years. Mo had liked him and it had seemed like Shereen was utterly in love. Whenever the camera caught her, she was looking lovingly at Stefano. So why hadn't they married? She'd always said she would be a writer first, then she'd get married straight away and start her family of six children.

Was the boy she met in her teens the reason she hadn't settled down? Shereen had refused to go into detail whenever Mo brought the subject up. Mo shook his head and wondered how she and Liam were doing. Pushing down the discomfort that rose in his throat at the thought of them getting back together, he took himself to bed.

Chapter 8

Shereen opened her eyes to a sunlit room, pain lancing through her head. She groaned, closed her eyes, and stayed perfectly still. It was a while since she'd had a hangover as bad as this. Instead of stopping when she was tipsy, she'd carried on drinking. Liam was a great drinking partner and a great friend. Whenever she had something she couldn't share with her group of four friends because she'd be skinned if she told one and not the other, she'd confide in him. He was great at keeping secrets too.

So they'd drunk and had fun. Like a sloth, Shereen peeled the sheet from her body, turned and put her feet on the floor. She wobbled her way to the kitchen, aiming for the medicine cupboard, and downed two paracetamol.

She switched the kettle on. Too tired to get a mug and the coffee, she sat down, resting her elbows on the table with her arms holding up her head. She wouldn't think about anything that happened last night until she'd ingested some coffee.

“Feeling better?” Her dad’s voice came from behind her as she sipped at the glorious brown liquid from her mug.

Shereen turned around to see her dad walking behind her mum, making sure she was okay.

“Why? Was I not well?” she tried to sound innocent. How long had it been since her parents gave her the third degree for coming home drunk?

Mum snorted. “You were well over tipsy when you came in. Good thing Liam brought you in. What happened to Mo?”

Shereen thought about her word choice. Her parents weren’t happy when she broke up with Liam. “Mo gave us some space, which he didn't need to do, and left early.”

“That was decent of him,” her dad said slowly.

Shereen caught the concerned glance between her mum and dad. *What’s with the weird vibe? Why didn’t Mum agree straight away with Dad?* Shereen knew they liked both Mo and Liam. In their eyes, surely both had behaved well—one helping his friend and the other trying to sort out his relationship with their beloved daughter?

Deciding to leave that question for later, Shereen finished her coffee. She looked at the clock. It was eleven twenty, and she had plenty of time to get ready. She cast her mind to the night before, trying to remember what she’d done. That’s right; she'd invited Liam to the barbecue next door. Shereen sat up, shaking her head. Why had she done that? Turning up with a man at the Rodrigos counted pretty much as declaring she was dating? What had made her do it?

She spotted Dad getting up. "Shall I make breakfast?" she suggested.

"Will you be able to do it?" Mum asked sarcastically.

"I will in a minute, when my head stops pounding."

"I'll do it." Dad pulled the bread out from the fridge.

"I'm going to lie down for a bit."

"Don't forget to put your alarm on," Mum called out as Shereen left the kitchen.

Shereen plodded upstairs and laid on her bed. Liam had said he was spending the whole weekend in London and wanted company.

"I can't, I'm attending a barbecue tomorrow, it's Mo's dad's birthday. Besides, you have tons of exciting friends you can have more fun hanging out with them." Shereen had brandished her wine at him.

"I'd rather attend a family barbecue; you know that. Besides, you're my friend, if I want to hang out, isn't it your duty to make me feel better? That's what I'd do if you turned up in my neck of the woods."

Shereen knew that was true. Liam was a good friend to her, so she'd agreed. It would be okay, she told herself, what was the worst that could happen? The Rodrigos would tease her about her boyfriend? She could handle that by setting the record straight.

She closed her eyes, waiting for the pills to do their work. When she opened them again, the alarm was ringing. She shut it off and headed for the shower, after which, another cup of coffee would be in order.

"Mum, do you need any help?" Shereen called from outside her parents' bedroom.

"I'm okay, dear," her mum answered.

Shereen sifted through the clothes she'd brought with her from Leeds, looking for something smart-casual. She decided on an okra-coloured belted dress and her favourite brown, lace-up platforms. Her hair, usually up in a ponytail, she straightened and left it hanging down her shoulders. After applying black mascara and eyeliner, she went with her favourite nude lip gloss.

"Are you ready?" Shereen called to her parents.

"You go on ahead. We'll see you there in a bit," came the reply.

Shereen looked at her watch. It was a little early, but she was nervous. When she was younger, the Rodrigo house had pretty much felt like home. She'd practically been part of the family. Rebecca had treated her like her own daughters, speaking to her in Portuguese, giving her chores to do, and teaching her to cook the same way she'd done with Maria and Sara. She'd called Mo's older sisters "mana", the Portuguese word for big sister, the same way Mo did. The family's friends had become accustomed to her too. But since she left home, apart from Mo's wedding, and his Uncle Seb's and Catarina's funerals, she hadn't spent time with the whole family the way she was going to do today.

Rather than wait for her parents, getting even more nervous with every passing minute, she'd made up her mind to go early and offer to help out where needed. She was only fifteen minutes early anyway.

There were cans of fizzy drinks and cartons of fruit juice in the front garden next door. "Help me bring those in," Mo called over his shoulder as he walked into the house. Shereen smiled as a sense of déjà vu assailed her. She picked up the remaining drinks and walked into the house, pushing the front door with a foot to close it.

Shereen followed Mo through the kitchen into the back garden where she placed the drinks next to a large tub of ice already filled to the brim. "Where is everybody?" she asked because the kitchen was empty. She stared at the large garden, just like her own. Rebecca had green fingers, so the vast lawn was edged by an array of flowers in a kaleidoscope of colours. But today, it was especially beautiful, adorned with balloons and banners, and the delicious and familiar smell of the Rodrigo brand of cooked stews, grilled meat, savoury pastries and cakes. The food was split between savoury and sweet—the main courses on a large table occupying one side of the lawn, while the desserts filled a smaller one opposite. "Are they still getting ready?"

Shereen turned at the sound of footsteps behind her. She smiled at the tall man walking towards her. Apart from the mop of white on his head, a few wrinkles on his face and the weight of age visible in his eyes, Mo looked exactly like his father.

"Hello, young lady," he greeted her, walking out into the garden.

Shereen kissed Mo's dad on both cheeks. He'd been out yesterday morning getting the drinks for today when she was helping Rebecca make the savoury pastries, so hadn't seen him for a few days.

"Let's sit and enjoy a few drinks in the quiet before everyone arrives." Uncle Zacchaeus said, taking a seat in the middle of the garden.

Mo and Shereen laughed.

"What's so funny?"

"You love the noise when everyone is here. We get it, you're trying to get a couple of drinks in before Mum comes down, but if she finds you drinking, Shereen and I will be the ones in trouble."

Shereen turned to hide a smile. Diagnosed with pre-diabetes, Zacchaeus had to watch his health closely over the past few years. Shereen sat to one side of him and watched as Mo grabbed a beer returning to sit on his dad's other side. Out of the corner of her eyes, she studied Zacchaeus, a little shocked by his entirely white mop of hair. Even though he was still a handsome man, there was no denying the man who'd given her piggybacks as a child, was ageing.

Shereen remembered those special occasions Zacchaeus played with her, Mo and the other Rodrigo children because those were very rare. He always seemed to be away working, and whenever he was at home, he'd be resting or watching television. At those times, Rebecca's strict orders were not to disturb him. The occasional picnic at the park, a trip to the beach, taking the bus to Central London for the tourist attractions and Sunday lunch after compulsory mass, which included Shereen when she'd spent Sundays with the Rodrigos were fond memories for Shereen.

"When can I read your next book?" Zacchaeus asked after taking a slow drink of his beer.

"You finished the last one only a couple

months ago!" Shereen glanced at him.

"Where are Alex and Zeke going next?" He asked about the female and male protagonists of her bestselling Alex Caddell fantasy series. Again, there was curiosity in the eyes directed at her.

Mo shook his head, a hint of a smile around his lips.

Shereen shot up. "The new book will be out in a few months. I think Auntie Rebecca is coming down now. I'll get you some food." She shot daggers at Mo as she passed him. He could at least have helped instead of sitting there laughing. He knew she found it hard to keep information from his dad. Zacchaeus only used to read biographies, but when she debuted, he tried her book out of support and discovered he loved young adult adventure stories. He devoured her books within days of receiving them and had started reading other young adult authors.

As Shereen entered the kitchen, Noah walked into the room with a woman that could only be Libby. "Hey, Little Girl." He kissed Shereen's cheeks and hugged her.

Shereen squeezed him back, feeling the strength in his arms and wondering why she wasn't the slightest bit annoyed at him for using the nickname he'd given her when he was three. Growing up, she'd bristled every time he called her that.

He pulled away and brought the woman beside him forward. "This is Libby, my fiancée. Libby, this is Little Girl—"

Shereen stared daggers at him this time. Using the name affectionately was one thing, introducing her as such was a whole other level.

"Okay," Noah conceded, "This is Shereen, my de facto baby sister who's been AWOL for most of the last decade. Rumour has it she lives next door, but she was always here."

Shereen kissed Libby. "It's nice to meet you." She'd been so curious about the woman that had made Noah Rodrigo settle down. There was a hint of red on her peach cheeks, but her indigo-blue eyes were clear, her expression open. Even though she only reached Noah's shoulder, she and Noah looked great together.

"You too, Shereen," Libby replied.

Shereen raised teasing eyes to Noah. "See, Libby remembers my real name after hearing it once."

Noah chuckled as he pulled Libby towards the garden. Shereen made to grab a plate but stopped when she heard Ben's excited voice.

"Auntie Shereen!"

She gathered him in her arms in a fierce hug. Had it only been a few days since she'd seen him last? Then she became embroiled in a greeting ceremony as Mo's five nephews and nieces, his sisters and Rebecca all greeted her. Now the barbecue had officially started. Eli came in soon after with his girlfriend Laura and Mo's brothers in law, and someone cranked the music up. The garden came alive with laughter, conversations and the fragrant scent of freshly cooked food. The party was well underway when the doorbell rang.

A little apprehensive, Shereen went to answer the door. Rebecca's old friends, Mama Isabel and Papa Pedro stood at the door, holding food trays. Shereen helped to bring the food in and then a little self-consciously, and feeling like the prodigal son, accepted their warm embraces and greetings as Isabel demanded to know what she'd been doing with her life.

Shereen was sitting with Libby and Sara, when Noah walked into the garden with Liam.

"Little Girl, I believe Liam is your man," Noah said, with a mischievous look in his eyes.

Shereen shot him a nasty look before giving them an official introduction. "This is Mo's brother Noah." Then, she turned to the group, "This is my *friend* Liam."

She took him to greet her parents and meet Rebecca and Zacchaeus. As she took Liam to the food table, Mo walked into the garden with Ben, a plastic plate in his left hand. Liam smiled and stretched out a hand to Mo.

Noticing Ben looking at Liam, Shereen picked him up. "This is my friend Liam. Say hi," she said.

"Hi Uncle Liam," Ben said. "I have two friends at school called Liam, but they aren't as big as you."

"I'm going to be even bigger when I've eaten my fill here. It all smells delicious. I don't know what to eat first."

"I can show you what's best," Ben suggested, wriggling to be put down before grabbing hold of Liam's hand and pulling him towards the food.

"You have a lovely son," Liam said to Mo over his shoulder as Ben dragged him away.

Shereen stood with Mo for a moment as the two of them watched Ben inform Liam what all the dishes were, then with a laugh, they followed and went to enjoy the food.

"So this is the Rodrigo home. You're so comfortable here. You must have spent a lot of time here," Liam said to her as he was heaping food onto his plate.

Shereen looked around at the groups of people chatting and nodded. "I spent a lot of my childhood here."

They sat over to one corner of the garden, but it wasn't long before Liam heard an opinion about politics he couldn't ignore. So he joined that conversation, and soon Shereen found herself chatting with Laura, Libby and Sara.

Soon after the cake had been cut, Liam left. It was starting to get dark as Shereen walked him out to the front gate, conscious of all the eyes on their backs.

“You made a lot of friends,” she said.

Liam slid his hands inside his trouser pockets. “They are an easy-going lot. I had fun. Thanks for letting me invite myself, but you should have warned me about Maria.”

Shereen laughed. “You enjoyed pitting your wits against her, don’t deny it.”

Liam chuckled. He stared back at the house for a moment before looking over to Shereen’s.

“What? Are our houses so beautiful?”

Liam shook his head. “They are. But that’s not what I was thinking.”

Shereen looked at both houses too, wondering what was on his mind.

“It’s Mo, isn’t it?” Uncharacteristically, he scuffed his shoes on the path looking down at his feet a moment.

“What?”

Then Liam looked into her eyes. “The man you’re in love with. The reason you couldn’t give your heart to me. It’s Mo.”

Shereen stared at him, shaking her head.

Liam smiled. “It’s okay, you know. Oddly, it

makes me feel better."

"We're friends. We've always been friends." Shereen's voice was small.

"Are you sure? That's not what it looked like to me. I'll see you soon." Liam patted her shoulder then shuffled off, hands back in his pockets.

Shereen stared at his back until she couldn't see him any longer. What had Liam meant? She'd never told him about her crush on Mo, so why would he say something like that? She sat on the brick wall fencing the house. She enjoyed spending time with Mo, and they were friends. She thought back to the time she spent with him and Ben, and the anticipation she'd felt every time they were going to meet.

It was true she'd been thinking about him more often. Was it only because of their friendship? She thought of the way her eyes found him first in any room, and how she noticed those ripped muscles of his. She shook her head.

"You okay?" Eli asked.

Shereen jolted from her thoughts in surprise. She hadn't even heard Eli's car pull up after he'd gone to get more ice. She nodded, then helped with two heavy bags while he carried in two more. "Are you sure you got enough?" she teased.

When she stepped out to the back garden, her eyes found Mo sitting with his father. She sat with everyone else, nodding here and there along with the conversation, but her heart was heavy as a scary thought took shape in her mind.

Later that night, Shereen let herself into her house and leaned against the front door. She shook her head, but the truth wouldn't budge. *I am still in love with Mo Rodrigo!* She meandered to the kitchen, switched the light on, removed a glass from one of the kitchen cupboards and poured water from the fridge's cold dispenser. Drinking it slowly, she stared at the pictures of herself on the fridge door—various school photos, one of her leaving for university, her graduation, and the release of her first book. At all those stages of her life, Shereen realised now, even when she thought she was over Mo, she was still in love with him.

She'd tried so hard to get over him during those first years away. She'd studied hard, attended clubs and, whenever she had a spare moment, she had taken to writing to keep her mind busy —anything to stop herself from thinking about her first love. When she'd finally stopped thinking about him constantly, she'd thrown herself wholeheartedly into dating and enjoyed it. After breaking up with Liam, she'd begun to wonder why none of her relationships led to marriage and children, which was what she'd wanted since she was a little girl. She wanted a loving husband and a house full of kids. So the fact none of her relationships were successful irked her. Given what Liam had said tonight, it all seemed to be her fault.

She still remembered how Stefano, her other long-term boyfriend, had looked at her when they broke up.

"You are not serious with me," he'd shouted, the accent he'd managed to control thick in his voice, olive skin stretched tightly over his aquiline nose and fire cracking in his eyes.

She'd grabbed his arm, saddened to see pain in his beautiful, golden eyes that had laughed with her so often. "Stefano, I care about you. Why would you say that?"

He'd groaned and snatched his arm away from her. Paced the entire length of her small sitting room, long legs eating up the space. He'd finally stopped in front of her. "Let's get married then. I have no choice. You know Papa is now sick, so I must go back and run our family practice. You can write anywhere in the world, come and live with me in Crete."

Even as part of her wished to say yes and bring back that joyous light into Stefano's eyes, another part of her recoiled and rejected the idea. Heart as heavy as lead, she blinked, trying to hide the confusion she felt. Isn't that what she wanted? Despite the fact he had many siblings, like her, Stefano wanted a large family and house. They had so much in common and always enjoyed each other's company. In every sense that she could think of, he was an ideal life partner for her. Moreover, Greece wasn't so far away that she couldn't visit her parents often, and they loved Greece.

But she'd stood there, agony lancing every fibre of her body as realisation struck—she couldn't bring herself to say yes.

She took his hands in hers and looked into his eyes. "I'm so sorry. Maybe I'm just not ready to get married. I'm only twenty-four." What was she saying? Since when did she consider herself too young to get married? Hadn't her dream been to marry anywhere from a year after graduating with children following every two years?

"Can you let go that easily?" He shook his head, brown curls flying everywhere. "I can't believe this. We've been together for four years."

Shereen recalled they'd been wonderful years, from the moment she met him during her second year in Leeds while he was doing his masters in dentistry until his proposal. It wasn't easy for her, and she was heartbroken. But, worse still, she hated hurting him.

"See, you are not serious about us." Stefano had freed his hands and stood staring at her for one more awful moment. Then, "Goodbye, Shereen," he'd said softly, stalking away from her.

Finished with the ice-cold water, Shereen almost crawled up to her bedroom. The emotions swirling in her mind completely sucked. Had she lied to herself all these years? She got ready for bed, going through all the motions, mind a blur and limbs heavy. Why the hell couldn't she get over Mo?

She switched off the light and flopped onto the bed. Was there any point in dating other people if she was doomed to repeat the same cycle? She'd only be hurting others and, ultimately, herself.

Shereen squared her shoulders. Enough of lying to herself. It was time to take control. She guessed she'd have to be like her main female characters. They might be younger than her, but they always took control of their love lives, no matter where their decision took them.

The problem was she didn't want to lose Mo. That hadn't changed. His friendship was too important, there was nothing she could do without risking it. She thought about their trip to the park, the moments they'd spent together lately. She wanted those moments to happen again, wanted to be a mum to Ben and a life partner to Mo.

There, she'd admitted that to herself, and it felt as if it fit perfectly. She wanted to be Mrs Mo Rodrigo, and have brothers and sisters for Ben.

She'd loved the last few weeks with Mo, and he couldn't deny that he'd enjoyed spending time with her too. There was no doubt in her mind about that. But, did he still see her as a sister, a childhood friend? Shereen lifted her hands and raked her hair, trying to loosen the pressure in her head. What was she going to do?

Hadn't she read somewhere that a relationship that began with friendship was a good thing? That was it, a relationship with mutual respect and shared goals, was more likely to last for life. Well, they had that going for them. There was so much they could give to each other. As far as she could see, the only problem was she wanted to get naked with him. But did he want the same? They enjoyed the hell out of each other's company. However, she hadn't seen any sign to show he was attracted to her. She couldn't live with just a platonic relationship. She couldn't see Mo agreeing to that either. He was such a virile man; he wouldn't want to be celibate for the rest of his life.

From their conversations, she knew he wasn't in any serious relationship. Now, his life was Ben, work, family and friends. However, that didn't mean he wasn't having sex. Shereen frowned. Was he? She didn't know everything about his life.

There was another issue to consider—Catarina. Ben's mum was still an integral part of Mo's life. But Shereen had noticed a difference in him and wondered if he'd started to accept. He wasn't the same person he'd been after the funeral or even a year ago. He'd started living again, although she wasn't sure how much Mo realised he'd started to accept Catarina's passing.

So, what was she left with? Did she have the courage to seduce Mo? She'd never seduced anyone as far as she was aware. All her relationships had been with men who'd found her attractive. So, how was she supposed to seduce her best friend? What if he was disgusted by her? Worse, what would happen to their friendship if things didn't work out?

This was the crux of the situation—the huge risk she'd be taking by confessing her feelings to Mo. Had this been the reason she'd run away from a possible romantic relationship with her teenager best friend? Yes, run away was the accurate term, for her actions all those years ago. She was still terrified, but now, she understood her situation; there was more on the line than her friendship with Mo. What would become of her life if she didn't do everything possible to fight for the type of relationship she wanted to have with Mo? If it was a disaster, she could move on knowing she'd tried, but if she didn't even try, nothing would change.

She grabbed her phone—eleven o'clock. Andrea would probably still be awake. She dialled her friend's number and held her breath. *I am really going to do this.*

"Hi dear," Andrea's zone out voice came over the line.

Shereen breathed a sigh of relief. "I know that

voice; you're Netflixing," Shereen said.

"Hmm."

"Listen, can you talk?"

A pause. Was Andrea pausing the drama she was watching? That was her thing. Andrea loved binging dramas. Mostly Korean and Chinese, a love she'd inherited from her Asian mum and aunties, but also Brazilian, Latin American and mainstream. Because of this, amongst her four closest friends, she was the go-to for dating advice. There was no romantic conundrum, Andrea didn't have a solution for. Whether that worked or not was another matter, but at least she was always able to give a suggestion.

"Okay, I'm all ears. What's happened?"

Shereen smiled. Her friend was such a gossiper. Her almond-shaped eyes were probably wide, the inquisitive light in them glowing.

"One of my friends had this friend, well male friend she had a crush on when they were teenagers. They both had other relationships, but now they are single. The woman still has a crush and is wondering how she could seduce the man." Shereen waited—and waited. "Andrea, are you still there?" she asked when she thought at least a whole minute had gone by without an answer.

"Sorry, Shereen. So this is about one of your friends?"

Shereen frowned. "Yes. One of the girls I went to school with," she stopped herself from adding, *I think I told you about her once*, in the name of not telling too many lies then forgetting what she'd said.

"Ahh. Well, seduction is the way to go, but it has to be subtle, so she doesn't scare him away but not too subtle he doesn't get the hint," Andrea said.

"How do I do that?"

"You? This is about you, isn't it?" Andrea's voice rose a notch in her excitement.

"What?" Shereen swore in her mind. What a klutz. "I meant my friend. What should she do?"

"Okay, it's about your friend." Andrea didn't sound convinced. "Tell her the first thing she must do is review the types of clothes she wears when she's around him. Go for more provocative clothes. Sensual rather than in your face."

Shereen thought about that. "You mean like, tailored dresses that cover everything but cling to every curve?"

"Yes. Do you know what type of woman our man likes?"

What was Mo's type? Shereen asked herself. As far as she knew, he'd only ever been with Catarina. She was incredibly smart, assertive, beautiful with large doe eyes. Every time Shereen had seen her, even the one time she'd come to visit Shereen's parents while Catarina was sporting her pregnancy bump, she'd been impeccably dressed.

"My friend told me he likes beautiful, confident and smart women."

"Hmmm," Andrea seemed to be thinking. "Is your friend like that?"

"Kind of," Shereen muttered, then cleared her throat. "She's kind of beautiful and smart but maybe not as confident."

"She's not too far from his ideal type of woman then. Tell her to create lots of opportunities where they are alone. If he's likely to switch friend to man mentality, the sexier clothes coupled with alone time will start to bother him in the nicest possible way. Tell her to try some provocative gestures as well. She could lean in closer than usual if they're standing together, wear a stronger perfume."

Shereen nodded along, then realised Andrea couldn't see her. "Should she try to go physical? Like kissing him?"

"No!"

Shereen winced.

"Absolutely no. Not at first. Your friend has to see how he responds to the clothes and gestures first. There's always a chance this won't work. Sometimes a man just won't be able to see a friend as a woman. It's no reflection on the woman. It's just biology. If he doesn't push her away, there is a chance. That's when touching his arm, or his chest comes in. Starting to create the mood."

"Hold on," Shereen interrupted. "By creating the mood, are we talking about music, wine?"

"Exactly. Tell your friend to invite him for a meal at her house. Does she live alone?"

"Yes," Shereen said. Should she tell Andrea everything? Then she could explain the difficulty of being alone with Mo when she had to consider Ben. But she couldn't tell her friends about Mo yet. Even though she was quite open with them, this was too new, too raw. She wanted to keep that tiny flame of hope hidden, was not ready to share it yet.

"They could sit on the couch, for example, and she can touch the back of his head or touch his arm and look into his eyes. Then let it go and move on as if it was an accident, and she didn't mean anything by it. Let him feel the heat without getting burned."

Shereen heard the excitement in Andrea's voice. She'd taken the role of dating advisor seriously.

"This should make him want more. Then, when she thinks he's ready to jump her bones, only then does she initiate a kiss or a more blatant touch."

Shereen sucked in a breath. "What if it's a mistake? And he pushes her away? What if this ruins their friendship?"

"That might happen." A sigh. "It's something your friend needs to be prepared for. If they have been friends for a while, what's made her think of confessing?"

Shereen looked at her hands. She'd become accustomed to the darkness in the room and the shadows flitting about. "I think she believes it's the right time. She's scared life might happen to them and take them to different places anyway."

"There's no point in doing nothing and then wondering what might have happened. Sometimes you just have to take the risk. At least you'll know you tried and can move forwards knowing you did your all." Friends to lovers was Andrea's favourite trope.

Shereen pushed her hair back. "I guess that's what she decided."

"How long have they known each other?"

"Since they were one," Shereen said, then added, "so she says."

"Hmm, if she's a school friend that's about the same age as us. That's a long time to be friends. So I get why she's worried about their friendship."

Shereen laid down after she hung up and tucked herself under the covers. She'd made the decision. From tomorrow she was going on the attack. Even though it was only a tiny part of her that believed she'd come out a winner.

Chapter 9

Mo bit into his sandwich and gulped down water. The rush of filling an empty stomach was a relief. At last, two hours later than his allotted time, he'd managed to sit down and have something to eat. It was nice to be in his office since the fan he'd brought in provided cold air that cooled him. He took another couple of bites before looking at Tae Joon, slumped in one of his patient chairs.

"Sorry I couldn't make lunch," he told his friend. He and Tae Joon were going to have lunch at one of the restaurants near the hospital, but complications with one of his patient's had kept him there. "Thanks for bringing me the sandwich."

"I'm happy to hear you say that. My late tab is far longer than yours."

Mo couldn't even remember the amount of times one of Tae Joon's surgeries had overrun due to complications.

Mo looked at his friend, brows raising. "You look beat."

Tae Joon groaned. "My father is in town."

"Ouch." Mo sympathised. A visit from Tae Joon's father was synonymous with headaches and pains. Not once, since they met at Oxford, had Mo seen him happy whenever his father was around."

"Is it still the marriage proposal and you working at your father's main Korean hospital when you finish your speciality?"

"What else?"

Mo had accidentally found out that the bright, unassuming scholarship student he'd become friends with was the son of a chaebol—a Korean billionaire who was the CEO of a large chain of private hospitals in Korea and globally. Currently, said CEO wanted the son he once abandoned to marry the daughter of a large pharmaceutical conglomerate to consolidate a multibillion-dollar business deal.

"What are you going to do?" Mo asked.

"That's something that is not even worth a thought." Tae Joon stretched his long legs, but the action must not have brought him relief because he sprang up and laid himself down on the patient bed instead.

Mo stared at the feet dangling from the end of the bed and shook his head. "Why don't you go and lie down in one of the beds in the dorm? There's no way you'll be comfortable here."

"No time. I have surgery soon."

"Want to spar tomorrow night?" Mo asked. He'd taken up Jiu jitsu a few months after Catarina passed. Tae Joon had done it since he was a child and had suggested it to him. After the first day, Mo had known it was for him. Tae Joon seemed to use it as a stress reliever.

"Sure." He sprang up again and tousled his hair. "See you later."

Mo watched him leave, eyes narrowed. There was no point trying to pry anything out of him. After fourteen years of friendship, he knew Tae Joon well enough to realise he wouldn't say anything unless he wanted to.

The next day, after an intense workout and a shower, Mo and Tae Joon headed to the bar opposite the dojo where they trained. Bar staff had pitched the soft rock playing from speakers spread around the room at a low volume, and though it was busy they could still have a conversation. They sat at the bar.

"San Miguel?" The bartender asked as soon as they sat down.

"Hi Sam," Mo and Tae Joon greeted him. They exchanged a couple of pleasantries, but after Sam served their drinks, he moved to a customer over the other side of the bar

"You are getting too good," Tae Joon said, flexing his shoulders.

Mo laughed. "You just don't like to concede anything. How is getting a couple of punches past you getting too good? Only you would think like that."

Tae Joon grinned, the white of his teeth flashing against the subdued light in the bar.

"Seriously," Mo said, eyeing his friend's hands, "Shouldn't you give up Jiu jitsu? What if your hands get damaged?"

Tae Joon shrugged. "I've thought about it."

Mo shook his head. Again, that was a conversation he'd leave for another day. He swigged his beer, enjoying the rush of the ice-cold drink down his throat. Ben was staying over at his mum's, so Mo had another couple of hours to chill before heading home and sleeping if he wanted to wake up tomorrow in a fit state for work.

"How is work?" He asked.

"Just as I like it—crazy busy.

They talked shop for a while.

"How is your mum?" Mo asked. He hadn't seen Tae Joon's mum for a couple of years.

"Stressed by my father's visit." Tae Joon shook his head. "I think he's leaving in a couple of days, so everything will be back to some sort of normality." Tae Joon took a long drag of beer. "How is your friend Shereen? You mentioned she's back in London for a while."

Mo frowned. "She's doing well."

"Why the frown?"

"What?" Mo asked.

"She's well, but you're frowning. Why?"

Mo passed his hand over his forehead. "Was I?" Loud laughter disturbed the sound of voices in the room. He looked in the direction of the noise, at a group of people sitting near the entrance, then stared at his drink. "Nothing in particular."

He thought back to that strange sensation he'd felt seeing Shereen with Liam at his dad's barbeque and shook his head. It was the same as the way he'd felt the evening he first met Liam. It was a familiar feeling, but there was no doubt there was something strange about it. Had that sense of overprotectiveness been more than he'd felt for his sisters? He was much younger when his sisters were dating so he couldn't remember exactly how strongly he'd felt.

But lately, Shereen was often on his mind—laughing in the clearing at the park, the way she looked sleeping at his mum's house, how she wouldn't talk about herself at the pub because he'd refused to do the same. He wanted to spend more and more time with her. Despite his love for his sisters, he didn't think about them in the same way he did with Shereen.

"She's changed. I'm going to spend some time with her while she's here and was wondering where she'd like to go. We'll probably just visit our old haunts."

Tae Joon's eyebrows rose. "She's a beautiful woman. Is she married? How did it go with the guy she was dating?"

Mo looked at Tae Joon. He'd met Shereen during Mo's graduation party. At the time, she had been dating Stefano.

Shereen is beautiful.

Mo had always thought that since they were little. She deserved a great guy. Tae Joon was a great guy, but, unfortunately, his family was not. Shereen was the type of woman who was too kind for her own good sometimes, and throwing her into the lion's lair that was Tae Joon's family didn't sit well with Mo. "She is beautiful, and she's single at the moment, just out of a relationship, but she'll find a great guy someday," he said lightly. He didn't see the need to tell Tae Joon just how long she'd been out of the relationship.

Tae Joon laughed. Mo glared at him.

"What are you laughing at?" Mo asked.

But Tae Joon just laughed harder.

***

Shereen gazed at the brand new blue skinny jeans and top she'd bought for today's outing and raked her fingers over her head. She, Mo and Ben were going bowling. No way could she wear a dress, which would have made it easier to ensure her attire was sensual. Were the jeans and top sensual enough? The jeans hugged her butt, but they were not indecent. To her, they looked nice, especially paired with the million-button shirt that outlined her bust while being relatively modest. It was a sleeveless top so her arms would be bare.

They would have to do. She looked in the mirror. Should she leave her hair down? She almost always had it up in a ponytail, so would that be too much of a change? No, Mo had seen it down a few times. He wouldn't necessarily think anything was up. She finger-combed the chestnut fall and was pleased that the flat iron had done a great job of straightening it. She took care with her make-up, trying to make it natural while still making sure it brought the best out of her hazel eyes and honey brown skin.

As she dressed, she debated whether she should wear her platforms or trainers. Heels made her feel more confident, and the extra height made her look a little more elegant and stylish, but she'd never gone bowling in anything other than trainers. Wouldn't Mo spot that?

"Argh!" Shereen pulled her hair, then remembered she'd have to change into bowling shoes anyway, so what did it matter?

A knock sounded outside her door. "Are you okay?" her dad asked.

Placing a hand over her mouth, Shereen told herself to be quieter. "I'm fine," she called out.

She decided on the trainers. Andrea had said not to do too much too soon, so she'd be cautious. At five foot nine, she was slightly taller than average, so that would have to be enough. She sprayed the new perfume she'd bought, a sexy blend of coffee, vanilla and gardenias.

Finished, Shereen looked into the full-length mirror she'd forced her parents to get when she turned sixteen. She hadn't become a femme fatale with a change of clothes, but even she had to admit she looked good. Whether her appearance would make Mo take notice of her as a woman was another issue, though. The main thing was she'd done her best.

She waved to her parents when there was a beep outside.

"Have fun," they called out.

But as she closed the door, she wondered whether that would be possible. Bowling was something she had enjoyed with the Rodrigo family when she was a little and then later in her teens with Mo and sometimes Eli. Today, however, it felt like she wasn't going for the game but for another purpose.

"Hi Auntie Shereen," Ben chirped from his booster seat in the back seat.

Lips lifting, Shereen turned and blew a kiss at Ben, feeling some of the butterflies in her tummy fly away.

"Has your school summer holiday started?" she asked.

Ben nodded. "It's a big holiday that lasts forever. It's going to be so much fun."

Shereen laughed. "What are you going to do?"

Ben held his tiny fingers. "I'm going horse riding, I'm going on trips with you, I'm going to make sandcastles at the beach, and—" His right hand hovered over the fourth finger as he scrunched his face.

Shereen looked at Mo, noticed the smile on his face. What did Ben mean by going on trips with her?

"You're going to spend a lot of time with your cousins, and you're going to have lots of fun this summer." Mo stopped the car at a pedestrian crossing and looked back at Ben.

The little boy's face cleared.

"Trips?" Shereen mouthed to Mo.

"Later," he mouthed back, then faced the road and pulled away.

For the rest of the short journey to the bowling alley, Shereen's mind whirled, trying to figure out what Ben meant. He was so excited, he chattered away about the friends and teachers he'd miss, and Shereen was glad all she had to do was nod and answer briefly. But when they arrived, she told herself Mo would soon tell her what that meant and decided to focus on her agenda.

"It's busy," she said after Mo had driven around the car park once.

"It's the summer holiday. Did you forget how busy this place is during the holidays?"

Shereen shook her head. "There's a space over there."

As they started to walk to the entrance, Ben held out his arms. Mo laughed. He grabbed onto one hand. Shereen held the other, and together, they raised him high before bringing him down and doing it again.

"Whee, I'm flying," Ben said.

Music, voices and the sound of balls hitting skittles greeted them when they entered the bowling alley. They made their way to the long queue to collect shoes and waited in line with other families. Shereen looked around, surprised.

"It's changed, hasn't it?" Mo asked.

The chairs, the carpet and even the paint were different colours. "I'm glad they changed the carpet. Remember how threadbare and worn it was?" Eli used to rub his feet in the holes. Everything was different, except for the overall feel of the place. *Just like Mo and me*, Shereen thought, hoping for good changes to come. So much about them had changed over the years, but that trust she had in Mo, the way she felt at home when they were together, hadn't changed at all.

"Are you still a size seven and a half?" Mo asked.

Shereen nodded. Had he spotted the difference in her makeup and the sexier clothes she was wearing? Apart from that odd look when she entered the car, there was no reaction from him. And she still didn't know what that look meant.

They headed towards their lane, each carrying their own shoes.

"This is it," Mo said when they arrived at a lane in the middle, besides a large group of young teens.

"I'll get a ramp for Ben," Mo said before heading off.

Shereen nodded, then helped Ben put on his shoes and put her own slightly large ones, glad there was something else that hadn't changed—they still didn't have size seven and a half shoes.

"Here we go." Mo placed the child helper in

front of their lane then put his shoes on.

"Who wants to go first?" Shereen asked.

"Me." Ben jumped up and down.

Shereen programmed the machine. "I'll go last."

She sat down and watched Mo grab a small ball and help Ben throw it. It shot straight down the middle and struck all the skittles down. Joy surged, and she stood up, clapping.

Ben turned to her and beamed. "Did you see?"

"You scored! Yeah!"

"I scored every time," Ben said when it was Mo's turn.

"Let's see how I do," Mo said, looking at Shereen.

"I wonder if you still have the magical touch." She watched as he stretched and bowled the ball, his body a graceful length of ripped muscles and strength. Shereen's heart missed a beat. Since that fateful summer, when she was fifteen and discovered she was in love with Mo, she'd be giddy every time they went out or spent any time together. Things that had seemed normal and hadn't aroused her interest in her in the past had suddenly changed. She'd become aware of his every move just as she was again now.

Heat warmed her cheeks, and she turned

around, pretending she focussed all her energy on celebrating with Ben when Mo's ball was a strike. Instead of seducing Mo, he was seducing her. She was the one getting hot and bothered while he looked calm and triumphant. Shereen grimaced, she wasn't sixteen anymore. This time she wasn't going to give up that easily.

***

"It's been a while since I've seen you bowl. Let's see what you can do now," Mo said. He watched as Shereen bent to throw the ball, arms loose and strong, her movements beautiful. She'd always been like that. But something was different. Had she always worn such tight jeans? They hugged her bum like a close fitting glove? Mo shook his head.

"Are you going on a hot date tonight?" he asked when she finished a middling score.

Shereen stared at him. Then shook her head. "Why are you asking?"

What could he say? The way your butt looks in those jeans makes the boys in our adjacent lane stare at you, and that's bothering me? How could he tell her he was finding their staring rude and disrespectful? Even worse, how the hell did he say he was also a little distracted by the sexy way she was dressed, to his friend?

"You look beautiful."

"You don't look like you mean it."

"I just don't want to lose you to our neighbours."

"What do you mean?"

"You have a few admirers," Mo said.

"It's my turn." Ben pushed the child helper.

Mo went to aid him. He felt Shereen's gaze on him. He supposed he just didn't like the idea of all those boys staring at her like that. He concentrated on helping Ben and enjoying the game. He reminded himself he was Catarina's man, was strong-willed and the attractive woman beside him was his friend. Soon Shereen would be going back to Leeds. He wanted to spend as much time as he could with her before she returned to her writing cave.

The solution to his problem with the youths next door was simple. Every time Shereen bowled, he stood beside her, blocking their view.

"You're rusty," Mo said when Shereen scored another middling score. "Your playing had improved a lot before you left for university."

"I haven't played since then."

"It shows."

Shereen laughed. "Stop being mean."

Mo shook his head. "I helped you a lot with your bowling. I'm a bit disappointed you didn't keep up."

"Sorry, Coach."

Mo smiled. "Here." He moved closer to her. "The positioning of your fingers and your grip on the ball is still good." He adjusted her shoulders, pushed her hips to adjust her stance.

"Ready?" he asked. His voice was low, throaty, and when Shereen didn't answer, he cleared his throat and tried again, wondering what the hell was wrong?

When she nodded, he started to let go but something barged into them. Mo straightened up, and lifted Shereen with him pulling her protectively against him.

"I'm so sorry, so sorry."

Mo looked at the red faces of the two youths in front of him.

"There are young children here, so stop messing around."

"Sure, sorry again," one of the boys said.

Mo watched as they moved closer to their lane.

"What did you do that for?"

Mo heard the boy who'd collided with him ask before their voices became entangled with the chatter of their group. He turned back to Shereen. "Are you okay?"

She nodded. Eyes huge, she stared up at him.

Mo stared back into her eyes. His arms were still wrapped around her shoulders. He pressed harder before he realised how tightly he'd pulled Shereen to him. With her so close he could clearly see the burst of green surrounding her pupils and the gold flakes on the outer part of her irises.

Fascinated, he leaned even closer and felt Shereen do the same.

"Daddy, are you okay?"

Mo blinked. He looked down at Ben, and nodded. "Okay?" he asked Shereen again.

"Yes."

Mo slowly released Shereen noting the slight pink to her cheeks. "Are you hurt anywhere?"

Shereen shook her head, heading towards the ball, which slid down the lane when it fell.

Mo frowned at her back, then a little hand grabbed his. Mo bent and picked up his son. "Are you hungry?"

"No. I want to go toilet."

"I'll wait for you, go. Promise I won't cheat," Shereen said as she came up beside Ben.

Mo searched her face. Her cheeks were back to their usual honey gold, her gaze clear. So he left with Ben for the gents. He chatted all the way there and back, but his mind was thinking about that —what should he call it? That moment of fascination he'd experienced. It wasn't the first time Shereen's eyes had wowed him. He remembered the first time he'd been interested in her eyes. He was four, and the light in Mum's kitchen had turned the brown and green in her eyes into a kaleidoscope of colours. This time, however, the fascination wasn't completely innocent, he realised. He'd have to revise his plan and be careful of his female companion. Mo was sure he would be okay; his love for Catarina and his friendship with Shereen were that strong, and he wasn't going to ruin either of those relationships.

Chapter 10

A week later, Mo took out two shirts from the wardrobe, held one in each hand and moved to the standing mirror by the window. He placed the white shirt in front of his body and considered how it looked against the black jeans he wore. After repeating this process for the soft grey shirt in his left hand, he returned it to the wardrobe and slid his arms into the sleeves of the white one, fastened the buttons leaving the top one undone.

What am I doing?

Checking which shirt would look better, leaving the top button open? That wasn't like him. He hadn't done anything like that since the days he dated Catarina. His current life was too busy for him to worry about things like that. Sure enough, from six o'clock this evening, he was on holiday and had visited Catarina, but he'd been on holiday before and hadn't bothered about what he wore.

Being on holiday just meant spending more

time with Ben, his friends and family. Like tonight. He was going to Eli's Salsa and Kizomba Club to dance, spend time with his friend Shereen, who'd wanted to go dancing. He shook his head and finished getting ready. There was nothing wrong with wanting to look good – for —himself. And it wasn't like a second shave, choosing a shirt and buying a new aftershave had taken a lot out of his time.

And the button?—perfectly normal. It was the hottest summer he could remember. Opening up one button would help him keep cool while still making him look decent enough. He grabbed his wallet and phone and headed to Shereen's house.

"Where are you going?" Ben asked when Mo called to say goodnight.

"Auntie Shereen wants to go dancing. She hasn't done it for a long time, so she asked me to go with her."

"Daddy, you're not as good as Uncle Eli, so you can learn with Auntie Shereen."

Mo chuckled. "You rascal," he growled, making Ben laugh. "Listen to Auntie Sara and go to sleep early."

"Auntie Sara said because it's the holidays, we can go to sleep late. So I'm going to watch a movie with Raquel and Jay. Auntie Sara made popcorn."

Mo hung up the phone soon after, but what

Ben said about learning to dance stayed on his mind. Having grown up with kizomba, he'd learned to dance it at a young age. But since books had always held more appeal, he'd never put in enough practice hours to become a master. Dancing at family gatherings was enough for him. Where salsa was concerned, however, he was a beginner. So he supposed he was the right person to help Shereen rediscover Kizomba and learn to dance salsa.

"I could have met you there," Shereen said as the taxi taking them to the club pulled away from the kerb outside their parents' homes.

"Why? It's only a short walk from my house to here, and we can share a taxi. We're reducing pollution and saving money."

She was wearing black jeans like him, but hers were softer with a snugger fit and her emerald off-the-shoulder top was the shade of the verdant flakes in her eyes. He stared at the familiar street of his home as he breathed in deeply, trying to shake away his awareness of her and how sexy she looked. Was she ready to date again? But that didn't make sense. Why would she dress up when she was going out with Ben and him? Besides, it was only months since she and Liam had broken up. She'd never been the type to move on so quickly from relationships. After breaking up with Stefano, it had been a couple of years before Shereen started dating again. She'd probably decided to change up her style just like he was taking a little more interest in what he wore.

"You're right." She leaned back on the seat. "Are you all packed?"

"Mostly. Ben's toys take up most of the space." He mirrored her pose, making a mental note to relax too.

"Did you buy those inflatable beds and ducks, again? The ones you got last year?"

"Ben loves lying on the inflatable bed and staring up at the sky or listening to a story. It's one of his favourite things to do."

Shereen smiled. "Like his father."

"Have you decided what you want to do when Ben and I come back?"

Shereen shook her head. "Remember those long walks we used to go on?"

"How could I forget? I'm sure we walked the length of England many times over." He gazed at her, convinced the look of mischief on her face was the result of her remembering how much she'd made him walk.

"You enjoyed them too!"

Mo snorted. But although biking was his favourite thing to do, he had enjoyed those walks he took with Shereen. She'd been so excited about the history of the areas they visited that it was contagious.

"Why did you bring that up?"

"I was doing some research and found out about this secret cult that existed in the fifteenth century. It piqued my interest. It seems they were based around London. The house they used as their headquarters still exists."

Mo smiled. Shereen's voice had changed, was now charged with an excitement he knew all too well. "You want to make that one of our trips?"

"We'd be walking for a while, and Ben is too young to walk for a long time. I thought I'd go by myself."

"I can carry him when he gets tired. Besides, because of all the biking and walking we do, Ben has very strong legs for a four-year-old. It'll be fun as long as we take breaks."

Mo watched Shereen as she talked about her idea to make the secret cult leader a villain of a future book in her Alex Caddell series.Her face fascinated him the way her expressions came alive. The taxi ride ended too soon, when they entered the small courtyard of a trendy pub in Wanstead. They walked through the lively pub to the large room at the back, where Eli and a couple of other instructors taught the kizomba and salsa lessons.

The room was already packed with people drinking, chatting or getting ready to start classes.

Mo spotted Eli at his usual table and headed over, greeting a few friends on the way.

"I'm going to have so much fun tonight," Eli said, his unusual green eyes full of mirth. "How long did it take you to learn Kizomba?"

Shereen shook her head. "What kind of teacher are you?"

Eli laughed a deep chuckle that had heads turning his way. He clapped Mo on the back then shepherded Shereen towards a stage at the back of the room. "This is where the salsa beginner class takes place. You're lucky to have Solange teaching you. She's not going to make fun of you like I would. But I'll be watching you from my spot," he said, then introduced Shereen to a tall, slender woman who shook her head at Eli.

Mo joined Shereen and the other people who gathered around Solange. After a quick introduction, they lined up in pairs, facing each other.

"Relax, it's just a dance," Mo said, noting the frown on Shereen's face.

"It's easy for you to say you've had a couple of lessons before."

"That was a while ago. I've forgotten most of what I learned, so we're practically in the same boat. And you're better than me at dancing, so I'll be the clown today."

Shereen laughed. "Only a little better, that it

makes no difference." She looked over at the dance teacher, saying something to another woman who was having her first lesson. "But I've wanted to learn for a while, so I am going to relax and think of this as fun."

They went through some basic steps without music. Having already mastered those, Mo didn't have to think about what he was doing and watched Shereen, ready to help her. She focused on the steps with so much determination, lifting her head up whenever her eyes lowered to look at her feet. Mo remembered doing that the first time he had a lesson. His lips lifted, and something warmed him. He couldn't help admiring her determination and perseverance.

Solange found a volunteer and demonstrated how to hold each other and the basic step. "Face your partners," she called out.

Mo took a step towards Shereen and held out his hands. Shereen closed the gap between them until only a breath of space separated them. She placed her left hand in his right and slid her right arm up his left until her hand rested on his shoulder.

"Like this?" She asked.

Mo breathed in as warmth spread along his arm up to where her hand touched his shoulder. The scent of coffee, vanilla and gardenias reached his nose, and he breathed in again, enjoying the captivating fragrance he'd come to associate with Shereen. He glided his left arm around her back, holding her firmly and looked into her eyes as Solange had told them to do. Shereen was looking up at him too, a question in her eyes. Mo realised he hadn't answered.

"Yes." Why was his voice rough? He cleared his throat. "We've hardly started, and I'm already thirsty."

"Me too." Shereen's voice was low and soft.

"Basic step on my count," Solange said.

Mo moved at the teacher's count, his lead strong so Shereen wouldn't have any trouble following. They rotated partners and danced with others until he returned to Shereen.

"I've got the basic step," Shereen whispered as she stepped into his arms, her dimples showing. "It's a little hard to keep looking into other people's eyes, though."

"We're dancing to the music. Keep the beat." Solange nodded at Eli, and the intermediate class teacher then pressed a button. A slow, soft beat sounded from the speakers around the room, and Solange started counting.

Mo glided back, pulling Shereen with him before gliding forward and repeating the movement, keeping to the song's rhythm and eyes on each other.

Shereen's holding my gaze just fine.

The thought entered his mind just as he noticed something else. The heat he'd felt when he touched Shereen, which wasn't there while he danced with the other women, was back. Did she feel it?

"Swap," Solange called.

Mo slowly released Shereen and nodded to the man that came to replace him. His feet dragged. Jealousy, he couldn't mistake that emotion anymore, reared its ugly head, but he told himself to grow up and pay attention to the woman in front of him. But as the lesson progressed, when he danced with Shereen again, and they tried out a few more complicated steps, he couldn't help noticing there was a frisson of more than the usual exhilaration of dancing with a partner.

During the club that followed the lesson, the main lights were switched off, and the disco lights came on transforming the room into a nightclub, with a small bar in one corner selling drinks. Mo and Shereen sat with Eli and some of their friends, chatting, dancing and drinking.

Shereen chuckled, and Mo watched her, noticing the way her eyes crinkled at the corners and how at ease she was in the large group. As a child, Shereen was timid and was more comfortable sitting in a corner with her nose in a book. As she grew, she became more confident, especially with friends and people she knew. The large gatherings his parents had at home were familiar to her, and at high school Shereen made more friends than in primary school. But she was still shy in the presence of strangers. The woman laughing beside him was confident, even though she'd only just met some of the people on their table.

They stayed until closing time and shared a taxi home. "I had so much fun tonight. I don't know why it took me so long to learn salsa," Shereen said outside her front door before she went in.

It was fun, Mo thought as he walked home, the moon in front of him and yet the sky still a clear blue. Having Shereen beside him had driven away the loneliness he'd started feeling lately, even when he was with his family and friends. She'd changed, was no longer the shy best friend she'd been when they were in their teens. She'd turned into a beautiful, attractive woman who was comfortable in her own skin.

His reaction to Shereen during the evening had revealed how he needed to be even more careful around her than he'd thought. However, he wanted to spend the time she was in London with her. The image of Ben asking to go toilet at the bowling alley popped into his head. That was it! His strong will, coupled with the safety of other people, was the answer. He'd go out with Shereen with Ben or his friends and family, he told himself as he entered his dark, empty house.

He readied for bed, sat in the sitting room and brought up one of his favourite pictures of Catarina on the TV screen. She was wearing her blue surgeon's overalls and was smiling at the camera. Her zest for life, the joy she got from her work were encapsulated in that photo.

When his eyelids drooped, Mo switched off the DVD and took himself to bed, reminding himself again of his promise to Catarina. He would enjoy spending time with Shereen while she was in London and would wave her off when it was time for her to return to Leeds. The tight feeling that constricted his gut when he thought of Shereen leaving London must result from not wanting to see his friend leave. As he surrendered to the darkness, the thought that he and Ben could visit Shereen once in a while slipped into his mind.

The next morning, Mo picked up Ben from Sara's house and went shopping for their holiday. They visited Catarina then spent the rest of the day packing his suitcase and Ben's.

"Wouldn't it be nice if Auntie Shereen could come with us?" Ben asked as Mo tucked him into bed.

Mo smoothed Ben's new, blue summer duvet, filled with images of horses. Earlier in the day, he had the same thought. "She's in London to spend time with Granny Rosa and Grampa Andy."

"Can she come next year? She'll love going on

holiday with everyone. Maybe Grandma Rosa and Grandpa Andy can come too."

"We'll see." Last summer, the whole family rented three adjacent villas in Spain and holidayed together for two weeks. Ben had loved it so much that he was looking forward to next year when they planned to holiday together again. "Are you excited about tomorrow?"

"I can't wait to go to the beach." Ben's eyelids closed, and he was asleep.

Mo smoothed the blanket one more time, amazed by how quickly his son could fall asleep. He switched off the light and headed for the sitting room to finish writing up the latest notes in his research and a paper, dragging himself to bed in the early hours of the morning.

Ben chattered the whole drive to the airport, getting through security and in the plane. He wanted to know all about Algarve. They arrived at the hotel around three, and by four, they were at the pool, the heat beating down on their backs. Mo laughed at his son's excitement and played with him in the pool enjoying spending quality time with him without worrying about work.

Ben made friends quickly, and they settled on a routine. Breakfast in the canteen in the mornings, a walk to the beach and making sandcastles before playing in the water, then lunch and a nap for Ben before afternoon kid's club and evening entertainment for Ben. When Ben was asleep, Mo spent his time reading medical journals and FaceTiming with Shereen.

The week flew by, and soon they were returning to the more temperate heat of London and their home. Mo had another week of annual leave and planned to spend it with Shereen, his family and Catarina.

He and Ben visited Catarina in the mornings and spent the afternoons at home in the garden or with family and friends.

"I'm ready, Daddy," Ben said one morning halfway through the week as he rushed into the kitchen. He turned and pointed to his backpack. "When are we going to get Auntie Shereen?"

"Eat your breakfast first." Mo placed a bowl of porridge on the table.

By the time they strolled off, rush hour was over, and the streets were quieter. Ben skipped forward and back to him, the warm early morning sun reflecting off the miniature horses on his new, shiny backpack.

"We're wearing the same trousers." He pointed to his faded blue jeans.

"Careful." Mo pulled him out of the way of a scooter.

"Sorry," Ben called out to the woman who'd popped on the pavement to avoid road works.

"We're a team, so we're in uniform," Mo commented, but it wasn't planned. He'd forbidden himself from obsessing over what he wore when he went out with Shereen. So, he'd grabbed the first pair of clean trousers in his casual clothes drawer.

"Maybe Auntie Shereen will be wearing jeans. Then we can be the three mouseketeers."

Mo chucked, enjoying the freedom to stroll down the street and the beautiful weather.

"There's Auntie Shereen." Ben pointed.

She was in uniform, after all. Patterned faded blue jeans covered her long legs, and she was wearing a t-shirt, just like they were, only different colours. A backpack was slung over her right shoulder. They reached her as she closed the small gate to her house.

"You're just as excited as Ben," Mo teased.

Shereen wrapped her arms around his son when he threw himself at her. Mo swallowed. She'd become a natural at receiving Ben's exuberant hugs. He realised then that he wouldn't be the only person in his house to miss her when she left. Ben loved listening to her stories and playing with her.

Grinning as wide as a Cheshire cat, Shereen held the hand Ben offered, and they set off to Hackney Central Station. It didn't take them long to reach Surrey Quays, where they'd begin their journey along the River Thames.

"Look at that big boat, Auntie Shereen." Ben pointed to a vessel with two floors, taking tourists along the river. He waved and whooped when a few people waved back.

They walked downriver for about an hour until they came across the Salt Quay Pub and the book shop beside it.

"That's it, isn't it beautiful. They only had to add a few reinforcements to it. Most of the original building was left alone," Shereen said.

The fire of curiosity had lit up in Shereen's eyes. "This is where you want to set most of Alex and Zeke's next adventure?" Mo asked, eyeing the ancient, stoned building.

Shereen nodded. "Hold on to Daddy," she said to Ben, then let go of his hand and removed a camera, notepad and pencil from her backpack. She placed the pencil behind her ear, the camera around her neck and snapped a picture of the building before moving off to take photos from different angles.

Mo's heart raced. Shereen looked ravishing in the provocative clothes she'd started wearing lately, but the little crinkle that appeared on her freckled nose when she was concentrating with total focus on a task and the pencil behind the ear unexpectedly affected him. Mo pulled out a water bottle from his backpack and drank deep until the bottle was almost empty. Then, bending, he offered the rest to Ben and watched as his son drank to keep his eyes from sliding to Shereen again.

"Let's go inside. What do you think?" Shereen asked as they moved towards the entrance.

"It feels old. The outside of the building is a perfect fit for the Alex Caddell Series," Mo commented, happy when Shereen smiled at him.

A few tourists were dotted around the shop perusing books. Mo held Ben's hand a little tighter as he followed Shereen. Books lined the walls to the ceiling. Old armchairs were sporadically placed around, and one corner of the large shop had a love seat with a soft rug in front of it. Portraits of people Mo thought might be authors lined any spaces not covered by books, and dated back centuries.

Most of the time, Shereen snapped the camera, but sometimes she wrote in her notebook. Mo's lips twitched at the fascination on Ben's face, who hadn't uttered a word for a while and was walking with his face uplifted, trying not to miss anything. Shereen stopped in front of a small door.

"Is that the door that led to the river?" Mo asked.

"It's sealed now." She clicked the camera.

In the past, the door had been camouflaged, behind it a secret passage to allow fugitives to flee via boat. That nugget had captured Shereen's attention.

They went up the narrow spiral stairs to the tiny space above. It was filled with books as well, and was even cosier than downstairs with a small sitting area. No one else was upstairs. Ben couldn't resist the bright orange sofa and let go of Mo's hand to plop himself there.

"It's so comfy, Auntie Shereen. Daddy, come and try it." He wriggled on the seat.

Shereen laughed as she dropped down beside Ben. "It's soft." She eyed Mo. "Come and try it."

Mo sat down and felt the soft fabric of the arm of the sofa.

"Selfie time. Squeeze in." Shereen directed her phone towards them and snapped when their three faces appeared on the screen. She stood up and meandered around, snapping like crazy again.

Mo looked at the pencil on her right ear. She'd forgotten to take it off before the selfie. A smile hovered around his lips.

"What's this word, Daddy? I sounded it out, but I don't know what it means." Ben pointed to a word in a large book.

"Where did you find a book about horses?"

"There." He pointed to the space on the bookshelf beside the sofa. "There's a picture of a horse here." He showed Mo the spine, which had a picture of a bay thoroughbred.

Mo read the horse's breed Ben was pointing to and listened to him read. He looked up when Shereen sat down next to Ben. A few more people had come upstairs, but they sat there for a while, Mo listening to Ben read while Shereen wrote in her notebook.

After a while, Mo realised Shereen was staring at him. Mo stared back. His eyes dropped to her rose lips.

"Excuse me," a man's voice said.

Mo's eyes lifted in the direction of the voice.

"I need to get a book from that shelf beside the sofa."

Mo stood and pulled Ben up. He grabbed their belongings and followed Shereen downstairs.

"Lunch?" Shereen's voice was bright.

"Let's go to the Salt Quay."

They ordered and sat in the pub's outdoor space, watching boats sail up and down the river. Ben brought out a small sketchbook and a pencil case from his backpack and began drawing the boats.

"Well?" Shereen asked as they waited for their food.

For a moment, Mo thought she was asking about the episode on the couch when he'd reacted to the look of longing in her eyes.

"Grange could use that old passage to escape the first time Alex and Zeke travel back for him!" The excitement in Shereen's voice was palpable.

"It's a great idea," Mo said. Had he made up the longing he'd seen in Shereen's eyes? The only interest in them now was for their expedition.

Let's focus on the trip and have fun.

"I don't think you should allow Alex and Zeke to discover the passageway until well over halfway through the book," he added. Grange was the main villain in the book. Alex and Zeke were enforcers from the future who travelled back in time to capture individuals that travelled unsanctioned into the past to change history.

They carried on discussing the book until lunch arrived. The rest of the day, they visited Brunel Museum and St Mary's Docks before heading back with a tired Ben.

Before he knew it, Mo's two weeks of annual leave were up. He'd managed to fit two more trips with Shereen, one a picnic with all his family and another a salsa weekend away with Eli and some of his friends.

He'd spent more time with Catarina too, and through the rest of the hot summer weeks, his plan to spend time with Shereen in the presence of friends and family worked.

Chapter 11

The streets were dark, lighted only by the moon and the pale light from the lamps above. A cold breeze blew past Shereen and Mo, stirring up the green-gold leaves on the trees and a carton of chicken and chips littering the road. Shereen shivered, her light jacket not strong enough to withstand the early autumnal chill in the air.

"Here." Mo placed his leather jacket around Shereen's shoulders.

"You'll get cold." She looked at his long-sleeved shirt. He didn't feel the chill as much as she did but still, it was cold. If they could walk wrapped up in each other, neither of them would be shivering, she thought. Shereen shook her head. She'd had a few too many drinks. Or she was tired of fantasising about kissing and touching Mo. She was ready to abandon her careful seduction. Instead, she breathed in the cold air, feeling it calm her wayward thoughts and bring her to some sense of reality.

They were coming back from a friendly drink at the pub, not a lovers outing. She'd been sending out signals, and there were a few times – the moments at the bowling alley, salsa club and bookshop – she thought Mo had been attracted to her, but they were always interrupted and afterwards Mo's reaction made her feel like she'd been mistaken. Going out with their friends, the way they'd been doing lately, didn't help the situation either. Eli and Tae Joon were supposed to meet them at the pub this evening, but both had cancelled at the last minute.

She was dressed in killer jeans again tonight, with a short-sleeved, maroon top that covered all her front and upper back but left a portion of her lower back bare. She'd taken her jacket off when they played pool at the pub, but she hadn't seen Mo glance her way once. Not even when she had to bend low to get balls placed at pesky angles on the table. Every time she looked at him, his eyes were firmly on the ball.

Maybe they weren't meant to be? Perhaps friendship was the highest their relationship could get to. But then she thought about the regret she might feel later if she didn't give a possible connection with Mo her best and squared her shoulders. She was going to try again tomorrow.

Suddenly, the skies belched out a downpour. Mo and Shereen sprinted the rest of the way to her house. With her hands slipping, Shereen struggled to open the door. By the time she rushed inside, rain dripped from both of them.

“What are you doing? Come in!” She pulled Mo into the porch, closed the door to the wet night and headed for the downstairs toilet. She came out with two towels and held one out to him, wondering what he was doing still standing in the porch.

“I’m going to dry at home. The rain will stop soon.”

“Don’t be silly. Why would you freeze when you can dry up and borrow Dad’s clothes?”

“I’ll go next door.”

“And wake up everyone?” Shereen threw the towel at him, removed her soaking shoes and rushed upstairs.

When she came down, after slipping on warm jogging bottoms and a jumper, Mo had dried his face and arms. She handed him one of Dad’s t-shirt and pair of jogging bottoms.

While Mo changed, Shereen headed for the cupboards, took out two mugs and placed them on the kitchen surface. Then, she switched on the coffee machine and put a teaspoon of sugar in each mug.

“How are your parents finding their trip? Can your mum move around freely?” Mo asked as he entered the kitchen.

“She has to go slow, but she can take short

walks and do most things. They are having fun. I don't think they want to come back."

"They can stay longer, can't they? They are both retired and your mum is not going back to her volunteer work for another month."

Shereen smiled. She served the coffee, handed a mug to Mo and moved to the large sofa in the open kitchen. She sat down with her legs crossed and sipped, enjoying the trail of warmth the hot beverage left as it passed her throat. She'd made up her mind to leave 'seducing Shereen' on the side and be the girl Mo seemed to enjoy spending time with, the girl she was comfortable being. His best friend that he could relax with.

"I'm here. I think they want to spend time with me before I go back to Leeds."

She felt Mo's gaze on her. "When are you going back?"

Shereen looked back at him. He hadn't started drinking yet. Was he warming up his hands on the mug? "I'm not sure. Probably in about six weeks."

About to take another sip, she halted midway. He was still staring at her. Did she have something on her face? Shereen placed her mug on the coffee table and looked back at Mo.

He placed his mug on the coffee table too. She waited, sure he was going to remove whatever was on her face. But something was strange. He hadn't taken his eyes off her when he put the mug on the table.

Still looking into her eyes, Mo moved closer. Shereen was powerless to move her eyes away from him too, feeling compelled to carry on looking at him. Helpless, she felt herself falling into the warm brown of his gaze. He sat down, put an index finger on her bottom lip, and then slid it from left to right.

Shereen shivered as a bolt of electricity shot through her. Her eyes widened and heat suffused her whole body causing her breath to hitch.

Mo leaned down, and Shereen watched longingly, as he moved closer to place his lips across hers.

It was like setting a torch to a mountain of paper. Sighing as if she'd been given water after a long trek through the desert, Shereen opened her lips. With the tip of her tongue, she licked the middle of his lips.

Mo groaned as he reached around to pull her flush against him. When he licked her tongue, tendrils of desire danced through Shereen. She pressed against him, ready for more.

Mo pulled back, cold air rushing in between them where there had been heat just a moment before. Shereen stared at him uncomprehending, wanting more, unable to hide the stark desire she was sure reflected in her eyes. Feeling naked, she stared into his stormy brown-black eyes.

Mo angled his head and pulled her closer again, this time crushing his lips to hers. Shereen opened for him, ready for whatever he wanted. When his tongue stroked hers she returned the caress, enjoying the thrilling sensation flowing through the whole of her body.

Mo's hands tugged at her jumper. She moved back a little, giving him access to her body, starved for his touch. Under the soft jumper, his hand caressed her stomach and moved devastatingly slowly up her sternum.

Needing air, not sure whether to focus on the sensations at her mouth or the fire igniting in her tummy, Shereen pulled away from Mo's kiss, the feel of his hands snaking closer to her breasts driving her wild. She leaned back and felt Mo's breath at her neck as he made a trail of tiny kisses up her neck.

Shereen held on tight, moving her arms to wrap around him. Mo lifted her to straddle his lap then kissed her again. Shereen placed her arms around his neck and stroked the back of his head when she felt both his hands snaking up her torso. She arched, sure she was going to explode in anticipation of that touch. Mo's large, slightly rough hands closed around both breasts and squeezed through the silky material of her lacy bra.

It feels as good as I imagined it'd feel.

Fire raced through to her core causing a moan to escape her lips, as she arched even more into Mo's muscular body. Breathing hard, she looked at him through the narrow slits of her eyes.

She'd never seen Mo like that. His eyes were on fire, his lips soft and delectable. He looked like a man who was ready to make love, a lover ready to have the best time with his partner.

Something cut through the fog in her brain. It was faint at first, but as she stared at Mo, it became louder. She became aware Mo had stilled and blinked. Finally it registered, her phone was ringing. Shereen looked at the kitchen island, where she'd left the phone and saw it vibrating. She looked back at Mo and swallowed. A chill ran up her spine.

The fire that had burned bright merely a few seconds ago was gone, replaced by something Shereen didn't want to acknowledge. She bit her lip, no longer feeling like she belonged on his lap. She moved off him feeling awkward. Getting onto his lap had hardly been a task she'd achieved on her own. He'd certainly helped. But now she felt every movement, as she scooted back to where she was sitting before this whole incident began with Mo frozen like a statue.

The phone stopped ringing. Shereen looked at her hands, laying limply on her lap. She couldn't hide. She didn't know what exactly had happened.

She'd thought her seduction wasn't working on Mo. But what happened showed that somehow, something had worked all right. She'd wanted this for a long time. But she'd never imagined this would end this way. Was it because they had had a little too much to drink? Regardless, this was her time to face her feelings, to tell Mo she'd loved him for nearly twenty years.

She took a deep breath in and faced him. If anything, he looked scarier now than when she'd stolen a glance at him before. She swallowed and in her hesitation, spied a little of what he seemed to be feeling. That emotion she hadn't wanted to identify was too strong for her not to acknowledge—confusion, betrayal, guilt. That much she'd been able to garner from the tortured depths of his eyes.

Mo stood up and walked to the furthest spot in the room, by the door that led to the garden. He stared at whatever was out there, the set of his shoulders hard. Shereen stood up.

"Mo," she started, wanting to hold him, comfort him. But if she was honest with herself, she also wanted to know if he felt anything else apart from those negative emotions. She pushed that to the side. Right now, that wasn't important.

"Mo, what happened—"

"I'm so sorry, Shereen. I have to go."

Shereen gulped. What was he sorry for?

Mo moved toward the door to the outside, but Shereen blocked his path.

"What are you sorry for?" She'd accepted that confusion earlier, but fear was starting to niggle at her. It was striking through her middle at an uncomfortable speed.

Mo rubbed his head and finally looked straight at her.

Shereen blinked.

"I'm sorry," he repeated, pain radiating from him. "I shouldn't have done that."

Shereen shook her head.

"The only woman I have in my heart is Catarina. I still love her. You're my best friend, I shouldn't have done this to you." He shook his head as if he genuinely didn't know how he'd come to be in her kitchen. "I'm so sorry, Shereen. I should have been stronger."

He shook his head and stared around the kitchen.

The fear inside Shereen had doubled the moment he said Catarina's name. It wasn't like she didn't know. She knew all too well that he still loved Catarina. She'd just hoped that maybe he was in a place to open his heart to her too. Was she wrong?

She opened her mouth to speak.

"I have to go." Anguish and pain rolled off him in waves. He stepped around Shereen and flew towards the front door.

Shereen called out to him, but he yanked the door open and slammed out. She stared at the door, shaking her head. That look of utter pain on Mo's face stopped her from going after him. She sat down, needing to take a moment. Because the fear she felt earlier was intensifying. She was terrified at what she had done to him.

Shereen wrung her hands. She wanted to go to him and explain. Tell him he hadn't done anything wrong, that it was all her. She called. The phone rang but there was no answer. Fear lanced through her once more as she put the phone down. Stomach tight, she placed the coffee cups in the sink and climbed the stairs to her bedroom.

Chapter 12

Mo stormed out of Shereen's house, mind a blur. He got into his car, started it but couldn't make himself drive. What had he done? How could he do that to Shereen? To Catarina?

"Mo!"

He looked up. Mum was calling him from the front door. What was she doing up?

Shards of glass tore at his throat. He cleared them, rolled the window down and leaned out. "I'll come back in a little while."

He reversed out of the drive and headed down the street. What the hell had just happened? A beep sounded, and he looked in the rear-view mirror. The car behind him was still beeping. Mo looked ahead and realised the traffic lights he'd stopped at had turned green. He drove on a little while but stopped the car. He recognised the street he was on and the fact that he wasn't safe to drive. Parking, he got out of the car and locked it. Then he tore out of there as if the devil himself was chasing him.

Mind a whirl, he ran as fast as he could trying to leave the turmoil inside him behind. He ran until his body was hurting, and all he could feel was pain. But when he returned home and showered, that image of him kissing Shereen was still imprinted in his brain.

Not just the image. The way she'd felt in his arms, pliant and soft, had made him want to crush her to him and never let go. He'd wanted to keep touching, and it'd taken all his strength to stop his hands wandering over her soft curves. The worst thing was he still wanted to be touching her.

He wanted to feel her soft, peachy lips under his at this very moment. Mo shook his head with a groan. He was her friend, for Pete's sake. But when he kissed her, it didn't feel like she was shocked, betrayed. The way her arms wrapped around him, her tongue had duelled with his almost in exultation. Neither thing had felt like she'd been coerced or was upset. Nor did he think she just hadn't wanted to say no to a friend. He couldn't stop feeling Shereen had enjoyed the kiss as much as he had.

Was that all in his head? Was he making excuses to justify his behaviour? He raked his hands through his hair. He wasn't sure he could trust his thoughts anymore. Could he even trust himself? If he loved Catarina, what was he doing kissing Shereen?

Picking up the phone, he dialled his mum's number.

"Are you okay?" the concern was clear in her voice when she answered straight away.

Mo took a deep breath in and exhaled. "I was in a bit of a hurry, that's all."

"Did something happen?"

Something that shouldn't have happened. I messed up. I trusted my strong will, but I guess I underestimated my feelings for Shereen.

Mo realised now that it wasn't just attraction he felt for Shereen. With blinding clarity, he realised how his feelings for her had steadily grown over the three months or so she'd been home.

"Mo?"

"Sorry, Mum. I'd forgotten something at the pub. I went to pick it up before they closed." It was a white lie, but she'd carry on asking if he didn't tell Mum something plausible. He knew she was concerned about him, but he didn't want her meddling. Besides, it was only a white lie, and if it meant she wouldn't be hurt by nurturing the hope he and Shereen might get together, this would benefit her.

"How's Ben?" Mo changed the subject

"Asleep. He had a wonderful time playing with his cousins. Your dad spoilt them."

Usually, that would make him smile. Mum was stricter than Dad where their grandchildren were concerned, but she spoilt them just as much as Dad did in her own way. They certainly spent more time with them and showed them way more affection than they had shown to him and his brothers and sisters.

"You spoil them too. Goodnight, Mum."

"I can have Ben tomorrow if you want to go out again."

Mo frowned. What was Mum playing at? The only person he'd gone out with lately, apart from his regular pub dates with Tae Joon and the few drinks he had with Noah, Bradley and Eli, was Shereen. Mum couldn't be having ideas already, could she? Not when Shereen was his best friend and his mum knew that. But it seemed like his heart didn't know that

"That's okay Mum, I want to spend time with Ben. Thanks, though."

"Okay, goodnight then."

Mo sat on the sofa and rewatched the video of his wedding. Guilt rammed at him and the longer he watched, the more it hurt. Seeing Catarina's smile, feeling the happiness that rolled off the screen hit him like a sledgehammer. Nothing could break the stone of guilt and hate towards himself not even the alchohol he desperately wanted right now. But Mo knew how to control himself, knew when he'd had enough so his ability to make decisions wouldn't be impacted. He and alcohol had developed that much of a relationship during the months after Catarina's death.

Mo made himself watch the woman he had betrayed, the woman he loved. Ben's mum. He listened to the promises he made and reminded himself of the joy he felt when his wife was beside him. When the video finished, he put another one on, this time a short video just before their graduation. Halfway through, he felt his eyes close.

The next morning, Mo woke up early and stretched to get rid of the knots in his shoulders and back. Then, he tidied the house and left for the cemetery fifteen minutes before it opened. "Good morning," the old man greeted him.

Mo replied and headed towards Catarina's tombstone, but now he was here, his feet dragged.

"I'm sorry," he said to her picture as soon as he arrived at her grave. He sat down and repeated the words, but the guilt wouldn't go away. He just didn't have a reason to explain what happened. And he didn't want to lie to Catarina. He didn't want to make excuses about being drunk. He'd messed up big time, and that made him mad and disappointed with himself.

He wiped a little smudge that had collected in the corner of her pictures and sat staring at the sky as if the answer to why he'd behaved how he had would be there.

After leaving the cemetery, he picked Ben up to go food shopping. His nephews and nieces had wanted to go, but since their parents had plans, his mum had thankfully quashed that idea. Mo didn't know what kind of company he'd be today.

"Did you have fun, Daddy?" Ben asked as Mo drove to the supermarket.

Mo tried to smile. He must have given Ben a satisfactory answer because his son carried on chattering. Mo nodded at spaces, only half listening. He tried to stop himself from thinking about what happened last night by focussing on work. Thinking about some of the research he was doing helped a little. His mind wondered to Toby. The young boy received his bone marrow from his mother the previous week and tried to be strong after losing his hair and feeling sick from the pre-transplant chemotherapy medication. They had done their best to minimise possible problems, but now they had to wait to see how his body would take to the transplant.

The supermarket was as busy as always, but it was the best time to go shopping for him and Ben. He picked up his son and placed him in the seat on the trolley. "It's getting harder and harder to fit you in here. It'll soon be time for you to walk and help me pick up the shopping."

"I like sitting here." Ben placed his hands on the bar of the trolley. "But it'll be fun to get vegetables for us. Especially clementines. They have a lot of vitamin C."

"Did you learn that at school?" Mo asked as he steered the trolley around two girls dancing in the fruits and vegetable aisle.

Ben shook his head. "No, Earth Mum told me. Daddy pick that one. It's greener."

About to pick a cucumber, Mo paused and looked at Ben. "Earth Mum? Who's that?" He picked the cucumber Ben pointed to and placed it in the trolley before moving along to the lettuce stand.

"It's Auntie Shereen. She's like an Earth Mum to me."

Mo froze. He made sure his voice was neutral. "What do you mean?"

Ben smiled. "It's easy, Daddy. Mum is my Heaven Mum. I miss her lots, and she loves me, but I know she can't come down to be with me." Ben looked at him but Mo just stared. "Freddie said when you get married, I'll have a mum. That will be my Earth Mum. So I decided Auntie Shereen is like an Earth Mum to me."

"Excuse me, can I get a lettuce?" a woman behind Mo asked.

Realising he was blocking the lettuce stand, Mo apologised, picked out a lettuce and moved away.

Mo looked at the excitement on Ben's face. His heart froze. How much was his son missing out on not having a mum? Before he started nursery, he never talked much about his mum. He seemed happy to go to the cemetery and enjoyed telling Catarina every little thing he'd done that week. But since starting school, he'd begun to ask questions, make comments—not many but enough to make Mo realise he was looking at other children's mums.

Mo did the talk, explained how his mum loved him but couldn't be with him again. He'd already had that conversation with Ben. Still, he reinforced it, by showing Ben all the things Catarina had prepared for him, the clothes she'd bought, the pictures she'd drawn on his bedroom walls and the videos she'd made during her pregnancy.

Ben had loved watching those videos of his mum. He knew what she looked and sounded like, but he didn't remember the warmth of her embrace. He didn't have any memories of being with her. Whenever Ben mentioned anything about missing Catarina, Mo had been gutted. That sense of unfairness would well up in him time and again.

Mo had explained to Ben that he could do all

those things for him, and he did his best to do all the things boys thought mums did. He'd read a book to him about there being different types of families. And for a while, Ben had seemed to accept that he'd have only a dad bringing him up while his mum watched over him from heaven.

What had changed? Was it spending time with Shereen?

"Daddy?"

Mo had stopped in the middle of the aisle causing people to manoeuvre their trolleys around him. He shook himself from his thoughts and started moving forward again. "Did Freddie use the word Earth Mum?" Freddie was Ben's friend from school.

Ben shook his head. "I made it up. It makes sense because I have a Heaven Mum."

Mo carried on doing the shopping, forcing himself to concentrate on the list he'd made. He cleared his throat. What should he say?

"You know how you said Freddie told you when I get married, you'll have a mum?"

Ben nodded.

"Well," Mo continued, "people get married when they love each other."

Ben nodded. "Like when Cinderella married the prince. You love Auntie Shereen."

Mo swallowed, that sense of confusion always simmering under the surface rose up again. He looked away from Ben, picking up something off the shelf he was passing by. Then he took a deep breath. Ben was his son and he couldn't afford to be spacing out on what to say. He had to concentrate on his son.

"You know how there are different types of love, right?"

Ben nodded.

"Auntie Shereen and I are friends." He thrust the vision of her soft lips, the desire filling her eyes and the memories of laughing and talking with her to the confines of his mind, forcing himself to focus on the conversation.

Ben screwed his face. "But you looked like you were going to kiss Auntie Shereen and only mums and dads, and girlfriends and boyfriends kiss."

"When?" Mo asked, confused now.

"When we went bowling. Did you forget?"

Mo looked at his son. How had he spotted that?

"When that boy bumped into Auntie Shereen, and she was about to fall, you stopped her. Then you looked at her for ages. And you were hugging her so tight."

Heat spread through Mo.

That was the first time I was distracted by Sher-

een's eyes.

Mo gulped. Ben shouldn't have seen that. "Did I? I was just worried she'd fall." Mo carried on with the shopping, glad he only needed a few things. "It's not something I thought about, marrying Auntie Shereen. I love your mum. What did the teacher say you're going to do on your next riding lesson?" He knew it was cheap, but he needed to get Ben off this topic.

Ben looked up. Mo could have kicked himself. The indecision in Ben's large eyes was almost palpable. He relaxed when Ben started speaking about horse riding. As Mo finished shopping, he made a mental note to keep an eye on Ben. His little boy wanted a Mum. Perhaps he could talk to a paediatric psychologist at work and get suggestions on how to tackle Ben's expectations?

***

Mo looked at Toby's parents, his heart going out to them.

"I know we'd hoped this wouldn't happen, but right now, he's in the best of places to get better. The doctors and nurses in the ICU are very experienced."

"It killed me to watch him struggling to breathe. I thought my own heart was going to stop. And everything was going well," Toby's mum said, tears streaming down her face.

Toby's Dad placed his arms around her. "How long will he need to stay in ICU? Can we stay in this room?"

Mo wished he could give the parents only good news. But the truth was he didn't know. "His blood results will give some indication of how his body is doing. But for now, the main thing is making sure Toby is out of immediate danger. He's in the best place for that." Mo looked at the picture of Toby's family on the room locker and the stash of colouring at the side of the room. The family had managed to brighten the sterile, specially ventilated room, which had been home to Toby and his mum for the last two weeks. The children's transplant ward was small with only had ten rooms, which meant they could have only ten patients at a time. "For now, you can stay in here."

Mo left the room and headed straight for the nurses' station. After checking a few files he carried on to his office. He'd finished his rounds for the day, and he didn't have a clinic in the afternoon. Feeling lousy, he forced himself to look at some of his research notes, but the words weren't going in.

Toby's smile, the way he was so intelligent and innocent at the same time, were going through his mind. Mo knew he shouldn't care so much for his patients, but it was hard not to. They all had their charms and were beautiful souls in their own way. Unfortunately, sometimes the children with leukaemia died if they couldn't find a bone marrow donor in time. And occasionally transplant patients died of complications; especially half-match transplants. Every time that happened Mo couldn't evade the pain that was left behind.

That night at the cemetery, he told Catarina what happened during the day then sat staring at the headstone. The silence that used to be comforting and companionable suddenly became swollen with a sliver of discomfort and uneasiness. Of course, it was his fault, but Mo didn't know how to turn things back to the way they used to be. He had betrayed Catarina with another woman. And he couldn't wipe away the guilt he felt.

He took his time with the routine of bathing and putting Ben to bed.

"Dad, you're squashing me," Ben said, trying to wriggle out of Mo's arms. Mo released him. "Was I?" He watched as Ben climbed into bed and pulled the duvet up to his chin. He stayed on the bed long after Ben fell asleep, watching the slight rise and fall of the duvet.

Halfway through watching another pregnancy vlog, Mo paused the video with Catarina's picture on the screen and just stared at it. He didn't know how long he sat there before the doorbell sounded, bringing him out of his spacing. He stood up, rushing to the front door so the person wouldn't ring again. He didn't want Ben to wake up.

Chapter 13

Shereen stared at Mo, taking in the shadows under his eyes. She'd put those there. "You didn't pick up my calls."

His eyes raked over her as if he was glad to see her. Hope and confusion battled for supremacy inside of her. Hope that maybe when he said he should have been stronger, Mo had meant he'd fallen for her and found it hard to resist her. Confusion because if that was the case, why hadn't he returned her calls. And why did he look as if he hadn't slept for days?

Mo stepped back.

Shereen walked past him but paused at the entrance to the sitting room. Catarina stared back at her from the TV screen. She was beautiful inside and out, Shereen admitted. For a while, when Catarina and Mo started dating, she'd been jealous. But when she realised their love was mutual, it was hard not to be happy for them. But Catarina wasn't here anymore, and Shereen had known her well enough to realise Ben's mother would have wanted Mo to be happy again. Still, she didn't want to have the conversation that was coming here.

"Can we talk in the kitchen?" Shereen turned to the kitchen. She declined his drink offer and sat down on a stool in front of the kitchen island. Mo stood opposite her.

An island separated them. It was as if the closeness she and Mo shared over the summer had evaporated. Shereen looked at her hands in her lap. They were tightly joined, the way she was holding herself tight, willing herself to be calm.

Mo was attracted to her. After what happened in her mum's kitchen, she didn't doubt that anymore. And he liked her as a friend. What she didn't know was whether his feelings went beyond just wanting to sleep with her.

She also couldn't help feeling he was ready to live life fully. And he deserved that. Yet, for some reason he was holding himself back.

She'd made her mind up to reveal her secret and had decided that if Mo didn't have deeper feelings for her, she wasn't going to wait for him anymore. She'd done plenty of that, and she'd heard somewhere that being rejected after a confession helped one to move on. But how did she tell her best friend of thirty-one years that she had been in love with him for half of their lives?

"I've had a crush on you since I was fifteen."

Well, maybe it hadn't been so difficult after all? Shereen looked at Mo. He hadn't reacted to her statement. Had he heard her? She'd rushed the words out, afraid of chickening out once again. She gathered herself, ready to repeat herself.

"What do you mean?" Mo asked, shock in his voice. The blank wall was gone, replaced by confusion.

Shereen took a deep breath. "Do you remember the time we went to the fair, on our fifteenth birthday?"

"The time I won a teddy for you?"

A warmth that he had remembered that precious moment of her life warded off some of the trepidation inside her. "Yes. That's when I realised I had a crush on you. That I was in love with you."

If possible, the shock on Mo's face increased. He pulled a chair out from the island and sat down. Still a cold slab of granite between them, but at least he was closer and listening to her.

"You never said anything."

And now, she regretted it. "I was afraid."

Mo's eyebrows rose.

Shereen shrugged, she was still afraid. "Your friendship was something I cherished dearly like a cosy blanket on a cold winter's night. If I confessed and you didn't feel the same way, things might have become awkward. The thought of not being able to talk to you, go out with you as a friend at the time was scarier than not dating you. I was terrified of losing you." Shereen stopped. She'd lost some of the closeness of their friendship anyway. Even though they were good friends, they had never been as close as they'd been before their sixteenth birthday.

"It never crossed my mind. I thought you were in love with someone else from school."

"You. I think deep down I've always been in love with you. That's why I couldn't fully commit to my relationships." Shereen shrugged again. She wanted Mo to know how she felt about him, how serious she was about him. That she would never have tried to seduce him if she wasn't willing to take a relationship with him seriously.

Mo raked his hands over his head.

Shereen bit her lip. "We were childhood best friends, Mo. I don't feel just friendship anymore. After the barbecue at your house a few weeks ago I realised I was still in love with you. That's when I decided I was going to seduce you."

"So the sexy outfits—"

"Yes." She took a deep breath. "I don't think you see me as just a friend either."

There was longing in Mo's eyes, and Shereen's hopes lifted. But then Mo stood, paced the length of the kitchen a couple of times and when he spoke, there was only anguish in his voice. "I'm so sorry I didn't know. That you were hurting because of me, and I didn't know it makes me sad. You were the best friends to me, and I clearly wasn't as good a friend to you." He took a deep breath. "You're right; I'm attracted to you. But I made a commitment to Catarina. I should have been strong that night, and I'm sorry I wasn't. You want a big family, and you deserve it. I'm not going to have any more children. I want you to find a man that can give you the kind of life you want."

Shereen swallowed. With just a few words, Mo crushed the tiny nugget of hope that had been growing in her. "Don't feel sorry, Mo. That's not why I'm telling you this. It was my choice not to tell you anything. And sure, when you started dating Catarina, it felt like my whole world was going to collapse, but it didn't. I was happy those years I lived in Leeds. I enjoyed my life." She forced a smile because she had been happy. "I wanted to do everything I could to give us a chance. Now, I can move on without regrets."

But she couldn't stop her heart from breaking into tiny fragments again. Tears stung her eyes, but she blinked them away. Standing up, she held her head high.

"Shereen, let me take you home."

Shereen shook her head, ignoring the conflict in Mo's voice. When he spoke in that tone, her heart leapt, believing there was a chance. But he wasn't willing or able to let go of the past and give them a chance, so for her own sake, she had to let go. "I'll be fine," she told him, then walked out of his house.

***

As soon as the door closed, Mo rushed towards it. He didn't want Shereen to leave. His heart a tangled web, he reached for the door to tell her he loved the way she made him feel alive, loved her laughter and the peace she brought to everyone around her; loved the sexy way she looked when she was focussed on work and was so proud of her for the brave way she'd confessed her feelings. He twisted the doorknob—

You made a promise to Catarina.

A tiny voice inside reminded him. Mo pulled his hand back, closed his eyes and pressed his thumbs into them. He had to be strong. He couldn't let his emotions rule him. That's how he'd hurt Shereen. The last few months he'd enjoyed spending time with her that he hadn't looked closely at what was happening to their relationship. There'd been a couple of times he thought he saw more than friendship in her gaze, but instead of careful consideration, he'd assumed nothing was going on. That he had become attracted to her, should have indicated to him that there was at least a possibility she might have started feeling the same way.

He hated hurting Shereen, and hated even more that she'd been hurting alone for a long time when he'd been completely unaware. Dragging himself away from the door, he headed toward Ben's room. His son was lying on his back with arms outstretched above his head. But looking at Ben only made him feel better as far as knowing his little boy was sleeping peacefully and his conversation with Shereen hadn't disturbed him. Because as soon as that thought registered, he remembered Ben's conversation about Shereen being like his Earth Mum.

Mo went downstairs and grabbed the skipping rope in the play area in the kitchen. Outside, he jumped until sweat entered his eyes and burned them and the drumming of his heart obliterated everything else.

But in the shower, his mind wandered back to Shereen standing in his kitchen with disappointment written all over her face. Did she believed he'd let himself down? Was he being less than he could be? The thought of her inviting eyes and arms on her kitchen sofa as she bravely gave herself to him was too much to bear. With a groan, Mo turned the water to freezing, the shock of the temperature forcing him to finish up and get out.

He forced himself to work every day. The thought of the children he might be saving was the only thing driving him forward.

A week later, he dropped into Tae Joon's office to pick up a book he'd been searching for. "How did you get this antique?" He asked, truly awed by the connections his friend had. There was almost nothing he couldn't find.

Tae Joon laughed. "It's who you know, isn't it?" He offered Mo a coffee doing a double-take as he looked at Mo, the mirth disappearing from his face. "You look like you did when you were an intern and hadn't slept for nights in a row. What's the matter?"

Mo shook his head. He'd sat down to drink the coffee and have a breather. The day ward had been busy today. "I've just had trouble sleeping, that's all."

"How's your new transplant patient? The young man."

Mo smiled. "It was touch and go a couple of days ago, but he's stable for now. His bloods are looking good too. So I think he'll be coming out of ICU soon."

Tae Joon whistled. "That was close. I know you worried you'd lose him. So," he scrutinised Mo's face, "what's wrong then?"

"Life," he looked at the model brain standing on Tae Joon's desk. "I thought I had everything figured out in my life, but it turns out that wasn't exactly true."

Tae Joon looked at the brain too. "That's life for you."

They sat in silence for a long time, sipping coffee and staring at that brain before Tae Joon spoke again, "Everything changes. Sometimes we must embrace the new things in our lives."

Two weeks ago, Mo would have emphatically denied that where his life with Catarina was concerned. But now he wasn't so sure anymore. He didn't know how, but Shereen had taken up residence in a part of his heart he hadn't realised he'd opened up to her. He couldn't forget the times they spent together, alone and with Ben.

That night when he went to pick Ben up, his dad was in the kitchen playing with him.

"Come up," his mum called from the top of the stairs.

Mo followed her, wondering what she wanted to talk about.

"I'm worried about you."

Mo looked around his parents' bedroom, trying to avoid his mum's penetrating gaze. "I'm all right. I've been busy at work, that's all."

His mum shook her head. "This isn't just about work."

Mo hugged his mum, but she pushed him

away. “Don’t try to wriggle your way out of this.”

Mo smiled. “I’ll be okay, Mum.”

“What’s happening between you and Shereen? Did you upset her?”

Mo stared at her. What did she mean? “I was unkind to her.”

His mum sighed. “Shereen loves you. I know she means a lot to you too. But, if you’re not careful, you’re going to lose her.”

Mo frowned. “Did she say something?”

“No. But it’s easy to see that in the way she looks at you and cares for Ben.”

Mo thought about his mum’s words as he put Ben to bed that night. Then he tried to look at photos of him and Catarina. He didn’t want to lose Shereen, he’d come to realise that. She was already in his heart, and he couldn’t let her go. He touched Catarina’s face, stared at it. His hand was still holding the album when the first rays of sunlight brightened the room and woke him up.

***

“Querida, I’m sorry.” Mo stared at Catarina’s name on the tombstone. “You’ll forever be in my heart. That will never change. And You’ll always be Ben’s mum.”

He pushed away some dirt that had fallen on the tombstone.

"Mo,"

Mo turned around. Catarina's parents stood a little distance from him. Tears ran down Catarina's mums face.

Mo stood up. With the back of his hand, He wiped his own tears and greeted them.

They stood, the three of them, side by side, gazing at Catarina. The silence was comfortable; they had done this many times before. They were used to mourning for Catarina together, as all three of them felt the grief of losing the precious woman she'd been. Catarina's dad turned to Mo. "You kept your promise to our daughter. You love her, and she'll live on in your heart, and in Ben long after we are gone. That's the promise you made her, to love her until you've drawn your last breath. And you're keeping that promise." He patted Mo's shoulders.

Catarina's mum nodded. "Opening your heart to another love doesn't mean you've stopped loving her. Your love for Catarina is in your heart, in the way you care about Ben. So now embrace life. It's what Catarina would have wanted. Don't make our baby into a bad girl." She smiled, Catarina's smile, large brown eyes shimmering.

Mo swallowed the lump in his throat but he couldn't speak. He nodded, finally understanding and accepting that his love for Catarina was part of him. It wouldn't go away because he loved someone else, loved Shereen. It was still strong as it had been all those years ago when he was sixteen and fell for her. It was just different, a purer kind of love, the kind that lasted forever.

He blinked back tears, trying to be a tower of strength for the father and mother who'd lost their only daughter and yet remained strong and brave. Kept going every day.

He nodded. "I won't forget Catarina. And I'll make sure Ben remembers her." He embraced Catarina's parents. For a long time, they stood like that, silent.

When they moved apart, Catarina's Dad looked at Mo again. "Live, for your sake, Ben's, and my daughter's. We'll come to visit your mum and dad and pick up Ben next week."

Catarina's parents always made the trip to England around this time of the year, and Ben spent two weeks with them. The first couple of years, they'd stayed with Mo, but after that, they began renting a house.

Mo looked back at Catarina's photo on the tombstone. "I'll be back," he said aloud. Then he headed out of the cemetery. He walked past the same tombstones he'd passed a thousand times, greeted the older man at the gate in the same way, but he knew this time was different to the way he'd left the cemetery ever since Catarina passed. There was a sense of emptiness in him, one that was both terrifying and exciting.

He headed straight to Shereen's house. Outside, he rang the bell. It was like he was sixteen again. Heart pounding, he waited for the door to open.

"Mo," Shereen's dad said from the hallway.

"Hi, Uncle Andy. I need to speak to Shereen."

Shereen's Dad looked at him, but he eventually nodded. "Shereen, Mo is here to see you."

"Come in," he said.

Mo entered Shereen's house feeling for the first time like a man coming to see the woman he loved.

"Hi," she said when she came down. There was an awkwardness in the way she stood that tore at Mo, knowing it was his fault.

"Can we talk?"

"I'll be back in a minute," she called out to her parents.

Mo waited until she started walking towards the front door before following her out. They went to the park where they'd played. A few people were walking their dogs, but otherwise it was deserted. Even the trees were bare, with only the most tenacious orange leaves hanging on. He followed Shereen to the swings and sat beside her.

When he'd left the cemetery, Mo thought he knew what he would say to her, but now she was beside him, he couldn't think of anything.

Standing, Mo moved to sit on the cold floor in front of her and stared into her eyes.

Shereen's lips tugged up into a smile that reached her eyes. "The fact that you want to cheer me up gives me hope I haven't ruined our friendship. But you don't have to do this, get up the floor is too cold. And I'm sorry I tried to seduce you. Considering our friendship, I should have been more open with you about the way I felt."

"I'm glad you did." Mo reached for her hands.

Shereen blinked. Her eyes drifted to their hands and back to his eyes.

"I am happy you did. Because that beautiful kiss, the moments we shared these past few months, helped me to realise how deep my feelings for you are. If you hadn't decided to seduce me, I don't know if I would have realised that I've come to like you as more than a friend."

"Mo."

"I'm sorry about the way I let you go that day. I couldn't see past the commitment I'd made to Catarina. But I do have feelings for you." He lifted a hand and kissed it, lingering over the soft honey gold skin.

Shereen shivered. Her eyes bored into the top of his head. "What do you mean?"

Mo let go of her hands. "I'm saying I wanna

get into your panties. And I want to hang out with you, do all the things we both love."

A blush spread over Shereen's neck and face. Mo watched as the combination of honey and rose stained her skin.

Shereen bit her lip.

"But I need some time. Can you wait a little longer for me?"

Shereen's arms crossed over her chest. "What are you saying?"

Mo stood up, shoved his hands in his pockets. He wanted to carry on touching her, but that wasn't right. He had to give her time, a proper explanation, and he wasn't fully ready to be with her yet. He sat back down.

"I know I love you." Fascinated, he watched as the gold around her irises darkened to almost a chestnut brown. He tightened his hands into fists to keep them to himself.

Be strong for Shereen's sake.

Clearing his throat, he tried again. For a moment, fear squeezed his lungs, but he pushed through it. Shereen had faced fear when she confessed to him. She'd exposed her feelings, faced the possibility of losing their friendship, to tell him how she felt. He could do no less.

"You know my life. I loved Catarina, and I still love her. That's not going to change." Was he asking too much of her? Mo didn't know; he just knew he loved her and didn't want to lose her. He had to find a way to make her understand—a way to put into words what he was feeling.

Shereen bit her lip and tightened her arms but didn't budge from her spot in front of him.

"It took a long time for me to accept she's gone. And it's taken even longer for me to realise that it's okay to love someone else again, to have someone else in my life."

Shereen reached out to him. "Catarina's passing isn't your fault Mo." She blinked back tears.

Mo breathed out. "Knowing in here—" He pointed to his head "—and knowing in here—" he pointed to his heart, "are two different things. But I've accepted that. Right now, I need time to say goodbye properly. There are so many things of Catarina's at home that I couldn't part with, and there's the way I've been living my life. I need to keep Catarina only in my heart, and I need time to adjust to that, so I'll be ready to come to you."

Shereen held his hand. "Let's sit on that bench." She pointed underneath a massive silver birch tree. Mo walked with her, glad she hadn't just rejected him outright. She was willing to talk, maybe make sense of the confusing words he'd said. He knew not every woman would be willing to take on a man who said he loved two women even if one had left this world. Saying it aloud had only made him feel like he was talking nonsense.

They sat down and watched a bird nearby fly upwards.

"This is what I'm hearing. You're fighting your way to me." Shereen looked at him. "Is that what you meant?"

Mo smiled and turned to face her. "Only you could put it that way." The smile left his face. "And I'm not fighting. That implies there's a chance I'll lose."

She pulled her feet up on the bench, crossed and tucked them under her. "You're sure you'll win?"

"Yes."

Shereen eyed him. She looked at his face, eyes roving over him. Then, after a while, she nodded.

"You trust me?"

Shereen sighed. "I do. You've never lied to me. You've been there for me every step of my life. But you have a lot to make up for. I know it's fate that you fell in love with Catarina first, but I'm still a little mad at you for that."

Mo swallowed. There was a lightness to the way Shereen spoke. But he was in awe of her. The way she forgave, the way she loved tore him to bits. The way she gave of herself, her understanding and how that had always made him feel safe and accepted finally hit home for him. That was what he loved about this woman. “I’ll spend the rest of my life making up for that,” he said, voice thick.

Chapter 14

Shereen looked at the screen. She was supposed to be writing, but nothing was coming out of her mind. The screen had a couple of words, but that was it. She looked at her outline on the magnolia wall in front of her and tried to focus. Pressing her hands on the keyboard of the laptop, she typed one word. A little while later, she found herself staring at the hundred or so words she'd written. Most of them didn't make sense.

She groaned and turned the computer off. There was no point in continuing like this, so she went downstairs to see what her parents were watching on television—a documentary about rallies in the seventies.

"Have you finished for the day?" Mum asked.

"Just taking a break. I'm going for a walk."

Shereen headed out. She crossed the road to take the path to the park. Children were playing on the swings, and the middle was full of groups of children playing football, but around the perimeter of the park, it was quiet. She walked laps of the park, trying to organise her thoughts.

She wanted to think about going forward, about her relationship with Mo but couldn't stop thoughts of the past from intruding. The memories bombarded her, like bombs, targeting her without permission. Reading alone in the garden while listening to the Rodrigo children play. They used to make so much noise. She always had her nose in a book when she was little. It was an activity she could do alone and still enjoy.

"Mum, can you play with me?" she'd asked one day when she'd been bored.

Her mum had cuddled her but told her she had to work. Her dad had tried more and whenever she told him she was bored and wanted to play, he'd play at least one round of a board game before going back to his work and giving her a book. She had so many books growing up that her parents had to give some away. She used to think she'd read all the books in the world.

She wasn't exactly unhappy, but she'd told herself she was going to have a big family, just like the Rodrigos next door. She used to dream of a mum and dad and six children. She didn't know why six, but that's what she'd always dreamed of. Maybe it had something to do with making sure her children always had someone to play with, the way it didn't happen at school. Sometimes there was an odd one out. She'd never liked odd numbers.

But now, she was contemplating having an only child. Not even considering, she'd kind of accepted Mo. And accepting him meant she might have to accept having Ben as her only child. Her lips tugged up when she thought of Ben. His large eyes were so like his mum's, the vivaciousness in them, the way he called her Earth Mum made her feel special; she couldn't deny that. Was it enough?

Warmth spread through her as she thought more about Ben. The way he held her hand. Washing him at Rebecca's house because he'd been so dirty after a messy day in nursery. She loved Ben like he was her own child already. She wanted to be his mother. Could she give him up because she wanted to have more children? Could she give Mo up?

Shereen shook her head. It wasn't because Mo had gone through so much, and she wanted to love him and take away the pain. It wasn't even because she wanted to give Ben a mum.

It's for my sake—my happiness.

She loved Mo. Sure she could live her life by herself or find someone to have more children with if she made her mind up to do it. But it wouldn't be what she wanted. She'd proved that to herself all these years since she left Hackney. She was happiest and the most complete when she was with Mo and Ben. And she wanted that happiness and fulfilment. So she didn't want to settle.

Even if it meant she couldn't have her dream of six children. Life with Mo and Ben was more important for her. They were her priority. This was a choice she was making for her happiness.

She didn't lie to herself, pretending she didn't wish Mo might change his mind about having children. She hoped he might, but she'd accept it if he didn't. She couldn't ask him to face the fear of losing her, not after what had happened to Catarina. That was something Mo had to overcome himself.

She headed back home, a new strength filling her. She headed straight to the sitting room, wrapped her arms around both her mum and dad and squeezed tight.

"Ouch, Shereen, what is the matter with you?" Mum asked.

Shereen squeezed a little harder before letting them both go.

"I love you," she said, turned on her heel and left the sitting room, smiling at the bafflement on their faces. As she walked up the stairs, it was as if the resentment and guilt she'd felt towards them washed out of her. The guilt she'd felt for resenting them had always eaten at her.

"Goodbye," she said to the little girl sitting on the stairs, nose in a book. She let it all go. Upstairs in her room, she thought about the box of tiny yellow and brown baby clothes she'd accumulated in the last few years and made a mental note to stop buying more. She wouldn't throw them away; she'd give them to someone who might need them.

Poor Ben, she thought, smiling. He was going to get a very clingy mum. From playing games, taking him horse riding, cheering at whatever sports he chose to do, helping with homework, showering him with clothes, she just hoped he was ready for all the love she would throw his way.

But one thing he wasn't going to be, was lonely, not even for a moment. Because Shereen had wanted to be a mum for a very long time. She'd prepared for it, made sure she could support her child and play with him. She could work whenever she wanted to. Besides, Ben had the Rodrigo family. And if she needed to, she could just have the little Rodrigos over and pretend they were one big family to satisfy that need in her.

How would her parents feel? Sadness washed over her. They wanted grandchildren; they'd started mumbling about that already. She knew they loved Ben but would they be satisfied with only him? Would they want to have a blood-related grandchild? Shereen didn't know. Telling herself she'd deal with that when the time came, she put all thoughts aside and told herself to focus on her novel. Maybe she could satisfy her need to have lots of children by writing about a family with many children? She smiled to herself as ideas flocked into her mind.

Shaking her head, she told herself to stop. She opened her laptop, checked her outline to see where to start and began typing, hoping this time she'd be able to concentrate.

***

Mo touched Catarina's favourite pandora necklace, moving his hands over the charms. Everything in the room brought back memories of her. That's why he'd kept her things. For those moments when he missed her physical presence, these were the things he could touch and remember touching while they were on her body. He'd used them to help keep the physical memory of her alive. He swallowed. It was time to remember her the right way in his heart. It meant he might forget some things about her, but he'd never forget her spirit and passion and the way they made each other happy by being devoted to each other.

He placed the necklace and her other jewellery in the box and moved to pack her clothes. There weren't many, but they each held a specific memory. By the time he'd finished packing, his heart was as heavy and dark as the darkness outside. He'd spent the whole day packing. Finally, he sat down on the bed, looking at their wedding and engagement rings. He couldn't help thinking of the happiness in his heart the day they married. Tears entered his eyes, and he blinked. He was going to be brave. He'd loved Catarina so much, that there was no way he'd stop thinking about her. She would always be a part of him. Feeling sad about how their life together ended would be with him for the rest of his life. He'd have to learn to deal with it.

He remembered a song his mum liked by Brazilian singer Roberto Carlos. Translated into English it was titled 'Woman of Forty'. It was a shout out to older women who'd suffered, maybe had a broken relationship in their past, who carried on living, happy but with a bit of pain inside them. They might shed a tear or two, thinking about the downs of their lives, but their experiences made them stronger and more able to deal with whatever came their way. The song was a celebration of the singer's love for women like that.

His mum and her friends loved that ode to the mature woman. He supposed he was like that in a way. He'd always carry the pain of losing Catarina, but he would find a way to live, even if occasionally he was down remembering her parting and the disappearance of the dreams their young souls had.

"What do you think?" Mo asked Ben after explaining what he was doing with Catarina's things.

"So Mum will be in my heart." Ben pointed to his chest. "And she will be in heaven."

"Yes. And we'll keep a few of Mum's things for

you."

"It's okay. Will I have two mums?" Ben's eyes were huge.

"Come here." Mo picked him up and hugged him. He blinked, swallowing the molasses in his throat. He'd worried about Ben's reaction before and during the whole time he was telling him about the changes he was making in their lives. Because everything he did affected his son. It wasn't just his life that was changing.

***

"Not that one, pick the yellow ones," Shereen's Mum said, pointing to a pack of bananas on the right-hand side of the banana box.

"Okay, Mum. Shereen put the fruit in the trolley. They were at Tesco, doing the weekly shopping. Her mum wobbled on a stick, but otherwise, she was fine.

"I know you are okay when you start to give orders. You've healed nicely." Shereen looked at Mum's foot and wiggled her brows.

"There's someone who's going to get something to heal if she doesn't stop getting silly." Her mum stared pointedly at Shereen. "Stop changing the subject. What's going on between you and Mo?"

Shereen sighed. There was no distracting her mother when she wanted something. She picked up leeks and aubergines, mind reeling, formulating an answer she could give her mum.

"Are you dating or not? I mean, for a while you were spending a lot of time together and while you've done that in the past, this seemed a little different. And you were happy."

Shereen bit her lip. "Am I sad now? Do I look that way?" She gazed at her mum, wondering how she looked to her parents.

Her mum gazed back at Shereen, her face pensive. "Not exactly. But you're not happy either. It's like you're waiting for something, I guess. Look, I don't know, that's why I'm asking, so hurry up and tell me."

"Mo and I are going to try to have a relationship." Shereen waited, looking straight at the ice cream cabinets.

When there was no response from her mum, she looked at her.

"Go on."

"I thought you might have something to say."

"What's there to say? At last, you're dating? You two belong together."

"We do?" Shereen stopped halfway down the aisle.

Her mum nodded. She picked up a tub of ice cream, threw it in the trolley. Then faced Shereen.

"You've loved him long enough."

"What does that mean?"

It was her mum's turn to sigh. "You've had a crush on Mo since you were in secondary school, right?"

"How did you know? I never said anything." Shereen had believed her mum was so busy and hadn't noticed the pain she was going through at the time. She'd also tried to be strong and bear everything on her own so she wouldn't disturb her parents. She thought she'd succeeded.

"The way you were with Mo, the happiness on your face whenever the two of you were together, it was the way I looked at your dad. I was like that when I was your age, utterly and helplessly in love. Your Dad was everything to me at that time. I didn't know for sure, but I guessed. So when I asked, and you didn't want to talk about it, I didn't push. I figured you'd tell me on your own time.

Shereen smiled. That was her mum. Giving her privacy to make her own decision, sort out her feelings. She'd loved and hated that at the same time, but now she was an adult, she was glad. She'd learned to stand on her own two feet. Shereen also realised her mum was there for her, in her own way. She smiled.

"I'm sorry I didn't tell you. So much was going on."

In a rare show of affection, Shereen's mum patted her back. Then she carried on walking. "Put the ice cream back. Let's have a coffee." She called back.

Shereen shook her head as she returned the ice cream and followed her. They parked the trolley and bought coffee and cake.

"You know you don't have to tell me anything if you're not ready, but I'm a little worried about you. I know you're happy with your career, and that's brilliant. I'm proud that you found something that you love and are passionate about. But Dad and I are getting older. I hate to admit it, you know I'm not the kind of woman to be knitting for grandchildren, but I want to see you settled. And I know that's what you want too. You're not the type of girl that would be happy living by herself."

Shereen looked out the window at a toddler sitting on a trolley chair, swinging her chubby legs. Her mum was right. She wasn't pleased about the possibility of living alone for the rest of her life. She trusted Mo and he said he'd come, so she was going to wait. He'd never broken any of the promises he made her. It's just that it was hard waiting and not knowing for sure.

She hadn't seen him since that day when they talked at the park, and that was three weeks ago. Spending time with Ben had made her feel calmer and happier. It had reinforced the decision she'd made, that she would be okay having one child if she could have Mo. And what a clever child he was. She couldn't help being proud of that fact.

"I believe Mo and I are going to be all right. We just need a little time."

Her mum narrowed her eyes. "Mo needs the time, you mean?"

Shereen nodded, remembering the sound of his voice when he spoke with her last week. "Do you think Aunt Gloria could learn to love again? Do you think it's possible to have a second love?" Her mum's friend lost her husband five years ago.

Mum wiped the coffee moustache from her lip and nodded. "Yes. I don't think it'll be easy, but she grieved, and now she's healing. I don't believe in destiny, that one is destined to love once or twice, you know that. But it's true some people don't ever love again, but others do. A couple of weeks ago, she was talking about signing up for a dating app. As if that's the right way to find a good man." Shereen's Mum scoffed.

Shereen laughed at her mum's expression. "There's nothing wrong with a dating app. A lot of people use them, and it seems to work just as well as meeting up casually. Some of those relationships last, and others don't. It's an easier way to meet people that are also interested in dating. It helps cut out a lot of time. Aunt Gloria is just more tech-savvy than you."

Mum shook her head. "The best place to find

a man is at church, weddings, family celebrations and through your friends. That way, you rarely get weirdoes."

"You're so old fashioned in some ways. It really cracks me up the way you're forward about women's rights and backwards where technology is concerned."

"Hey, don't make fun of me. I'm seventy and proud of it too. Some of the things you youngsters do, the way you do them, well it just can't be compared to the real experiences we had."

Shereen laughed. "You're priceless Mum."

"But you're smiling."

"I'm sorry I've made you worry. But really, Mo and I are going to be okay. I was just worried because the pain of losing Catarina hit him hard, destroyed a part of him. So I'm worried about the pain he's going through letting go."

"Mo is strong. I watched that boy grow, and he's as tough as a person can be. As much as I worried for you when he and Catarina got married, I had to admit they were happy. Maybe fate exists after all. Perhaps Mo was meant to have two loves in his life. She was the love of his youth, and you're the love of his future."

"You believe in fate?" But warmth spread through her. Her lips tugged up. That was a nice way to look at Mo's and her relationship. Maybe she needed to date and go through the pain of separation, again and again, to know Mo was the man she wanted to have in her life. So what did that make her? Was she a one man woman? Someone fated to love only once?

She shook her head. What did it matter? She couldn't predict life, predestine the future. Besides, it was hard enough to deal with the present.

"What are you going to do about your house in Leeds?"

She'd dreamed about what she'd do if she and Mo got together. She'd sell it and move to London. Yes, she'd made a life for herself there and moving would be painful. She'd miss her friends, their regular dates, and Leeds itself. But her parents were in London, and so were Rebecca and Zacchaeus. She wanted to be closer to her parents, and although her dad hadn't said as much, she knew her parents missed her. She'd make sure Ben never had a lonely childhood, but that family network would benefit him immensely. And she could adopt Mo's nephews, who technically would be hers too.

"I haven't decided. I'm going back in a couple of weeks. I have to resolve a few things. And honestly, at the moment I'm focussing on my work. Even though I didn't realise it, once I admitted I was still in love with Mo when I came back to London, it felt like I'd been waiting for him all my life. I don't want to overthink, I'll wait."

"Okay," her mum said, her eyes so much like her own, full of compassion and understanding.

Two weeks later, Shereen looked around her bedroom, taking in the same quilt she'd used fourteen years ago and all the things she loved before she left for university a broken teenager, including Fluto. These last few months, her life had changed. Again. She'd come to London worried about her mum, fear the only thing driving her. But she was leaving with her heart in a different place. Happiness was where she was. For her mum's recovery, the understanding she'd gained about her parents and the love she'd rediscovered. Also, she'd finally painted her bedroom magnolia.

She knew what path she wanted to take in her love life. Found a strength she didn't know she possessed and risked everything Mo's friendship meant to her. She didn't know how long she'd have to wait for Mo, but she'd wait. It was what she wanted to do, her choice.

She walked out of the room, closed the door and headed downstairs.

"Call us when you get there," Dad said.

How did Dad never tire of saying that? She used to tell him she knew, but she was quiet this time. For the first time, since she'd started travelling away from them, she was worried about leaving them.

“I will. Mum be careful, don’t rush, take your time doing things. You’ve really got to stop dashing around like a busy bird.”

“Who are you calling a busy bird? Just go, we will be fine.”

Her mum wrapped her arms around Shereen and squeezed tight. “You know I’m terrible at goodbyes, so I’m going back in. Drive safely.” She walked in, slowly but completely unaided.

Shereen smiled behind her back, glad her mum was okay. Her dad hugged her too and watched as she got in her car and put her favourite podcast on. She looked at the Rodrigos house, remembering saying goodbye to Rebecca, Zacchaeus and Ben earlier in the morning. Smiling, she waved to Dad and pulled out of the drive. She drove past the park, Mo’s voice as he told her he needed time ringing in her mind and startled when the phone rang. She looked at the screen of the car showing who was calling. It was Mo. Butterflies suddenly flying in her tummy, she hit yes to take the call.

“Mum said you’re leaving."

Shereen frowned. What was that accusatory note in Mo’s voice?

“I’m going to Leeds. I’ve been away too long. There are things I need to sort out.”

“Shereen—” There was a beep, and then someone was asking Mo a question.

Shereen waited, wondering why his voice sounded upset or perhaps disappointed.

"You promised to wait."

"And I am. But I'm going to do it in Leeds. And I really have things to do. You didn't think I would just up and go and not keep my promise? I would have told you if anything had changed."

"Do you have to be in Leeds by a certain time? Can we meet? I'll come to you."

Shereen blinked. "I'm driving. I just left Hackney."

"Okay, I'll meet you in Finsbury Park. Remember that place we used to go to? You can still park there."

Shereen drove, thinking about what Mo wanted to tell her. She'd given him space, believing it was best that way.

She waited at the car park, not wanting to go in and miss Mo. The Park was huge and had many exits. She passed the time by remembering the time they'd visited the park, the way they had been so happy there.

She spotted Mo walking towards her, a few metres away. Her breath hitched at the sight, reminding her of just how much she loved him. Loved the way he strode, like the road belonged to him. Loved his body and how her own body trembled when he was near her. She put her hand on the door to open it and get out, but it was too late.

Chapter 15

Mo yanked the door open and sat in the passenger seat. Then stared at Shereen. Just let his eyes roam over her as his heartbeat slowed to a regular rhythm. He wanted to hold her and crush his mouth to hers, and he barely managed to stop himself. It wasn't fair on Shereen. Not when they hadn't talked. When he hadn't told her he was ready.

"What's happening?" he asked instead.

Shereen looked at him, then turned to face front. "I'm going to sort out a few things. I was going to call you when I arrived."

"When are you coming back?"

"I don't know yet. In a few weeks, probably. I'm spending Christmas down here, so before then."

When his mum told him she was returning to Leeds today, he panicked. The worst entered his mind. He thought Shereen had tired of waiting for him. And his heart dropped. All he could think about was getting to her. Luckily he had no morning clinic and was able to get away. "How have you been?"

Shereen turned to him then. All huge eyes and that smile that gave her the two dimples he'd started to find sexy.

"I've been spending time with Ben. And my parents."

"He hasn't stopped talking about you."

Before he knew it, his hand was halfway across the front seat. He pulled it back. "I want to have a serious conversation, but all I can think about when I look at you is kissing you."

Shereen's face turned a cute soft pink. "I have a scarf in the back seat. Should I blindfold you?

Mo laughed. "That wouldn't work. Your scent is all around me. It's driving me crazy."

It was Shereen who laughed now.

"Let's get out of the car." No way could he remain inside and not touch her. So they sat on the bonnet. Mo breathed in the biting, mid-November air and looked over at the bare trees and shrubs in the park to distract himself from how beautiful Shereen looked today. He was genuinely baffled. He'd been her friend for so long, and although he'd seen she was a beautiful woman, it was only this summer that he'd found her irresistible.

"I'm sorry I haven't spent time with you. I wanted to give away Catarina's things and make sure I was ready to come to you." He'd needed to spend time with Catarina, had felt he owed it to her. He'd needed to get used to not having all her things in the house. That feeling of emptiness and also anticipation that surrounded the house after he'd given away Catarina's belongings had taken some getting used to.

"And now, how are you doing?" Shereen looked at Mo.

Mo looked back at her. Pride filled him and tugged his lips up. Because he loved her unwavering eyes and the determined set of her shoulders, she was so brave, and he had to be too. He couldn't let her down. Shereen had always wanted children. He couldn't let her not have the big family she wanted because of his fear.

"I am ready," he responded just as softly as she'd asked. "To be honest, I have been for a little while, but I know how much you want children, and I'm scared of losing you. I know the chances of what happened with Catarina repeating are slim, but it's a fear that is all too real for me."

"It's alright Mo. I would be happier with you and Ben than having a million children with someone that is not the man of my heart."

Mo shook his head. "Do you remember how often you made me play mums and dads when we were little? We had six children."

Shereen shook her head. "That was then. I've

grown up. I know we don't always get the things we dreamt of when we were young."

"You're right. But you deserve your family of six. I don't know if I'll have the courage to try for six children, but I'm going to be brave. Just like you." He'd been thinking about this for over a week, but his stomach became a ball of knots when he said the words. Still, he was determined to fight this battle for her. He wanted children with her, though six was a big number, he'd give at least three or four children a go. He watched as Shereen shook her head.

"I'm ready." He wanted that look of uncertainty gone from her face. He wanted her to know her dream was his dream too.

They stared at each other for what felt like a long time until the beep of a car horn sounded.

"You are?" Shereen said, slowly this time, as if she was starting to believe.

"Would you like to go out with me, Shereen Beckley? I'm bringing a lot of baggage and a precocious four-year-old boy. Can you put up with us?"

Tears ran down her face. "I'm in love with that precocious little boy, more than I am with you, you know," Shereen said, wiping them away.

"And me?" Mo asked, searching her face, eyes tracking the path her tears had taken. He'd put her through so much, had disappointed her.

"Since I can't have Ben without you, I'll have to date you then."

Mo pulled her to him, happiness spreading through him as her arms wrapped around him. He looked at the smile on her face, kissed one dimple, then the other. He kissed along the tracks of her tears, tasting the salt. Then he moved his lips to hers. Instead of crushing them to his the way he'd started dreaming of, he kissed her softly. When he felt her pressing back against him, he ran his tongue over the seam of her lips, until with a sigh, she opened them. Still holding himself back, he slid his tongue inside hers. Delight filled him as she met his tongue with hers and pressed tightly against him. His arms tightened around her and pulled her closer.

A whistle rang out. Cursing, Mo pulled away from Shereen and held her at arm's length. Colour, a bright red this time, spread over her face as if a fire had warmed it.

"I guess being outside isn't safe either," Mo said, waiting for his thundering heart to quiet. A rueful smile spread over his face, and warmth bloomed in his heart when he saw it reflected on Shereen's face. Feeling as young as a teenager, he let go of her hand.

"Let's sit a little apart from each other," Mo said and scooted a little away from her. Shereen did the same until she was nearly at the edge of the car's bumper. Then she scooted back to him.

"I don't want to be apart. Not even a little way."

Mo snaked his arm around her back and shoulder. "This is okay, and we won't get any whistles." It was more than okay, he thought, feeling the warmth of her body alongside his. He'd missed this. Sitting this close to a woman he loved and just staying that way. It was enough for now."

"What time do you have to go back?" Shereen asked.

Mo looked at his watch. "Too soon. I have a clinic this afternoon. I can make it back if I leave in about one hour."

Shereen burrowed further into him.

"It's going to be damn hard having a long-distance relationship," Mo said.

"I've decided to move back to London."

Mo pulled away from Shereen. He looked at her, a frown marring his face. Guilt a loaded gun in his chest. "You've built a life for yourself in Leeds."

Shereen cocked her face. "Aren't you happy we can see each other when we want to?"

"What are you thinking? Do you have that little faith in me? Do you think I was messing with you, that I wasn't committed to you and our relationship?"

Pink washed over Shereen's features. She

shook her head and pulled completely away from him. "You just threw me with that question. I guess I'm still sensitive. It's hard to believe we're together after so long. And I know how hard it's been for you…" she petered off.

Mo stretched his arms and held her by her shoulders. "I always loved the person you are, and all that's happened now, is that love has transformed into the kind of love a man has for a woman. I'm not about to let you go."

Shereen looked at his face, blinked twice, then nodded.

"What I meant is," Mo continued, "have you thought it through? It's not an easy decision to make, your friends are there, and you love Leeds. I'm selfish enough to be glad you'd willing to move here, but I'm not so wrapped up in myself that I can't see this would be hard for you."

"Don't tell me you thought it was only because of you?" Shereen asked, eyes that mischievous colour they became when she was teasing him.

"It wasn't?"

Shereen shook her head. "You really think I'm so in love in love with you that I'd be willing to do anything to be with you?"

Mo narrowed his eyes.

"I did it for Ben."

Mo smiled. He leaned forward and kissed her

forehead. "Thank you." He hoped she felt all his sincerity, his love and admiration for everything she was and the love she gave to him and Ben.

Shereen leaned back into his side. "I would have moved back eventually regardless of what happened to us. I think Mum and Dad need me, and I want to be close to them. They've lived in our beautiful house way longer than I lived in Leeds. Besides, although I love Leeds and wouldn't have minded settling there, this is my home."

Mo nodded. The guilt slipped away. There was so much he had to make up to her, he didn't want anything else adding to that list. But she'd given him a great gift. If necessary, he could move, but he didn't want to take Ben away from his grandparents and cousins. He'd always hoped his children would grow up with family around. And if he and Shereen ended up having more children, it would be great to have both their families around as a support network.

"I can't help feeling you're more in love with Ben. If I didn't have him, I don't know how I'd get you to give me a chance, Earth Mum."

Shereen chuckled. "That's right. What does Earth Mum mean?"

Mo explained Ben's concept. "I guess I should ask him for advice on charming you. It's been ages since I've dated."

Shereen laughed.

“Are you busy this weekend? We can come up to visit.” Mo suggested.

“I’d love that.” Excitement burst through her. She was finally dating Mo Rodrigo.

S[illegible] wa[illegible]

was as if [illegible]
weather was concerned. November in Leeds was way colder than in London and even though Shereen had layered up and was wearing a thick beanie pulled low over her ears, the cold still penetrated her body. She pushed her way into Pizza Hut and breathed a sigh of relief as warmth enveloped her. Tinsel and multicoloured lights glittered everywhere, giving the interior the spirit of the festive season. Shereen spotted her friends almost immediately, sitting by the window in the far right corner of the restaurant, waving at her.

Grinning, she marched to the table. "Sorry, I'm late."

It took a while to hug everyone, and by the time she sat down, a few tears had been shed. She wiped her face and looked again at her friends, [illegible] She'd never been [illegible] of weeks and had

[illegible] make me tear up again," [illegible] ing her sleek black hair be-

[illegible] ving Ivy has made me emotional," [illegible] wiping tears.

[illegible] een, Andrea, Heena and Kate burst out [illegible] ng.

"Don't blame this on little Ivy. You were already emotional way before you had her. Especially just before your period," Heena said, causing another round of laughter.

Sophie's premenstrual moods were legendary, and they'd been worse when they all met in their first year of university. Before the end of that first year, they'd found a five-bedroom house and rented it for their last two years at university. Living together, they had all taken turns preparing her a hot water bottle during the first day of her menstrual cycle when she was in agonising pain and as sick as a dog.

"Why didn't you bring her?" Shereen asked. She'd been looking forward to seeing the little girl.

"I wanted a proper girls' time out without worrying about nappy changes and bottle feeds. My mum is babysitting," Sophie answered. "It feels

so good to be out of the house without my baggage." She lifted a small black and purple tote.

"How did the meeting go?" Kate asked, her blue eyes holding Shereen's.

Shereen covered her face, trying to create suspense, but she was too happy to hold it in. When Andrea pulled one hand away, the smile on her face gave her away.

"They renewed the contract? How many books?" Heena asked.

"Three!" Shereen was late because the meeting with her agent and publisher had been delayed.

Andrea whooped, Kate clapped, Heena banged a knife on the table while Sophie hugged Shereen.

"We're celebrating with prosecco," Kate said. "I knew they'd sign you up. Your books are making way too much money for them not to. I wouldn't be surprised if someone wants to make them into a film."

"I know the perfect man to play Zeke. Dave Peterson. Isn't he gorgeous?" Andrea asked.

"Nope. He's too old, has too much brawn." Kate shook her head. "Zeke has a leaner build."

Sophie laughed, the sound a deep, unrestrained Irish melody. "Seriously, do you two just read Shereen's books to drool over Zeke's muscles?"

"What's wrong with that?" Andrea asked.

"I'm starving. I'm getting some food." Heena stood up and headed towards the salad bar.

Shereen followed Heena. She realised how hungry she was when she saw the slices of warm flatbread on display. Heaping her plate, she returned to the table to find Kate and Andrea still arguing about who would be best to play Zeke.

"What do you think?" Kate directed the question at her.

Shereen popped a cherry tomato in her mouth and chewed slowly, considering the question. Of course, she'd dreamed of her books being made into films, but that was as far as she got. She'd never thought beyond maybe. She'd just hoped she could write books people loved to read while making a decent living in the process. "Zeke's muscles are leaner but he's kind of a nerd. I think it has to be someone who looks a little nerdy."

Kate and Andrea shook their heads and headed for the buffet. Shereen caught up on her friends' news, enjoying chatting with them. They'd finished three large pizzas and had a few glasses of prosecco when Andrea's gaze arrowed in on Shereen. "Spill it. Who's the man?"

Four pairs of eyes focused on Shereen.

"Come on, that story about your friend needing seduction advice was really about you, wasn't it? And you said things worked out with the guy, so what happened?

"I'm dating." Shereen told them about Mo. She'd never meant to keep it a secret. When she'd first arrived in Leeds, her pain was raw, and she'd wanted to escape it. Making new friends and building a new life for herself was her priority and she'd avoided talking about Mo so she could forget her crush. As the years passed and her pain lessened, Mo became her childhood best mate to her friends, and Shereen hadn't seen a reason to change that.

But now, she told them the whole story.

"You must have missed him so much that first year. I can't believe you didn't breathe a word." Sophie hugged her.

"Wow, I'm so thrilled you got your happy ending." Andrea sighed.

"I just love how you're already kind of part of their family. It's like you are fated." Kate said.

"Plus, you've always wanted children. You can dote on Ben as much as you want," Heena added.

She would miss her friends, Shereen thought again as they left the restaurant and headed for their favourite bar.

***

Mo gazed around Shereen's cosy sitting room full of colour, from the bright coloured cushions on the couch to the pictures on the walls and the scattered souvenirs she liked to collect when she travelled. Her home was so much like her, warm and welcoming.

He and Ben had arrived so late the night before that he'd only stopped briefly at her place to see her before they went to their hotel.

"Daddy, come help make breakfast," Ben called from the kitchen.

Mo headed there and laughed when he saw the patches of flour on Ben and Shereen's faces.

"Things got a bit messy," she said, beating what looked like pancake batter. "I'm not used to making so much food all at once."

"Do you have an apron?"

"That third drawer on that cupboard to the right of the cooker." Shereen started cooking the pancakes. "This seemed like a great idea when I thought of it." She helped Ben scoop the mixture into the pan and decided to concentrate just on the pancakes.

Mo stood next to her, frying the eggs, bacon, tomatoes and mushrooms.

"It's yummy, Auntie Shereen."

"They are okay," Mo said, teasing her.

Shereen shook her head. "Ben likes them. So do I."

It was so good to see her. He hadn't realised how much of a comfort it was to know she was just around the corner. Now she wasn't nearby, and he missed her like crazy. FaceTiming daily helped, but it wasn't the same as being like this with her.

"You're staring," she whispered to him.

"I missed you," he whispered back.

"You've said that," she answered, but a smile played around her lips.

Mo forked another bite, enjoying sitting at this small table with Ben and Shereen. It felt right. He hadn't dated for a long time, and Catarina was the only woman he'd ever been with. Dating wise, he was sure he'd make mistakes. He'd pondered whether to book a hotel for a long time until he'd finally decided on it.

He hadn't wanted to put her on the spot, but when he mentioned he'd booked a room, she'd asked why he'd done that when she had a guest room in her three-bedroom house. Now he was wishing he hadn't, even though they had the whole day ahead of them and it would be a while before he and Ben had to return to their hotel.

But he had Ben to think about. His relationship with Shereen also affected his little boy. Even though he couldn't see anyone apart from Shereen in his future, he couldn't rush their relationship for his son's sake. That was also the reason he brought Ben with him instead of leaving him with his parents, or one of his sisters. He didn't want Ben feeling left out, not at this early stage of his relationship with Shereen.

They finished breakfast, and Mo washed up while Shereen and Ben found a game to play. “We’re playing twister,” Ben said when Mo entered the sitting room.

“I’m not dressed for that game. You can’t really play it with jeans.”

Ben lifted his leg. “I can move in my jeans. They are stretchy. Do you want to borrow Auntie Shereen’s jogging bottoms?”

“No!”

“I have a baggy pair. I’m sure they’ll be very comfortable,” Shereen said, shoulders shaking.

“I’ll try to play in my clothes.”

They took turns being the spinner. Mo was laughing by the time they gave up, exhausted, all three of them prostrate on the floor.

“I can’t make lunch,” Shereen said.

“We can go out.” Mo wanted to stay in, was enjoying being at home with Shereen and Ben.

“Let’s order takeout. I’m too tired to shower and get dressed.”

They had Chinese and spent the afternoon watching movies and eating popcorn. For dinner, they made hot chocolate and ate the bolinhos and bajan fishcakes his mum and Auntie Rosa sent Shereen. When Ben crashed just before seven, Mo picked him up, headed to the spare bedroom and laid him on the double bed there. Shereen followed him even though she'd given Mo and Ben a tour of the house when they first arrived. She watched as Mo switched the bedside table lamp on and left the door open.

"Just in case he wakes up," he said.

Back in the sitting room, they sat close together. Mo wrapped his arm around Shereen and pulled her closer. He leaned over until his lips touched her forehead, then pulled back a little. Shereen sighed and placed her head on his shoulder.

"Now that we're official, you know you'll have a hard time getting rid of me if you ever get tired of us. Our families just won't have it. They are claiming they got us together."

Shereen laughed. "How did they arrive at that conclusion?"

"Eli, my mum and Sara were arguing over who had the most influence on us getting together; they let slip their sordid deeds, which they are calling 'blessings'."

Shereen's head lifted.

"It seems Sara had offered to keep Ben with her so Mum could go to the retreat with Dad. But Mum thought if you did it, we'd get to spend time together and might realise we were made for each other."

"Auntie Rebecca is formidable."

"You wouldn't say that if you didn't want to get hitched and she was trying to arrange a marriage for you." Mo remembered the pains Noah had gone through to avoid his mum's arranged marriage schemes.

"What did Eli do?"

"Remember all those missed pub dates?"

Shereen nodded.

"The reasons were fake. The night of the downpour? Even Tae Joon got roped in."

Shereen shook her head. "And Sara?"

"The day she and I were supposed to take Ben and the twins to the cinema, and she called you for help, there was nothing wrong with her. I really can't believe my family sometimes. Especially Eli. It won't be long before Mum moves onto him to marry Laura. I wonder how he'll feel then."

"There's nothing you can do about Auntie Rebecca. Did you confront Eli?"

Mo looked sheepish.

"What did he say?" Shereen asked, intrigued.

"We were the only people that didn't know how we felt about each other."

Shereen looked at Mo. They both burst out laughing.

"I won't get tired of us," Shereen said when they'd sobered up. She looked into Mo's brown eyes, “I waited more than a decade for you. I’m not letting you go.”

Mo looked back into Shereen’s eyes. “I might get scared,” he said, still not sure how he was going to handle trying for more children, “And might need to take things slow, but I don’t plan on letting us go either.”

Epilogue

"Stop fussing, girl. You look beautiful already. There's never been a more gorgeous bride. I'm not saying that because you're my daughter, it's true," Shereen's Mum said, eyes shining with unshed tears. "And I don't know why these tears keep coming. They are going to ruin my make-up."

"You're biased, Mum," Shereen said, but she felt the same way about the tears. Hers wouldn't stop coming either. She'd already had to touch up her make-up a couple of times. It's just that it was hard to believe she was here, getting married to Mo Rodrigo, the man of her dreams. She'd been dreaming about this moment since she was a little girl. It had taken so long to get here that now and then, she pinched herself to check she wasn't dreaming.

Shereen's Aunt Gloria walked into the room. "Come on, you two, this is a wedding. And right now, all I'm hearing is nostalgia and sadness. I can hear music coming from next door. This is such a happy occasion. Let's put some bright music on to get you two out of the doldrums."

Auntie Gloria pulled out her phone from her velvet, grey blazer pocket, pressed some buttons and a few seconds later Donna Summer was belting one of her famous songs.

Shereen smiled. She'd grown up to seventies music; it was in her heart. Her mum started singing. In just a few minutes, the room was alive with singing and tapping feet.

Shereen's Dad popped his head around the door. He looked dashing in his tailored, black suit and bow tie. The grey beard and hair just gave him a distinguished look. His eyes rested on Shereen, "Are you alright?" He mouthed. Shereen nodded. Glad Auntie Gloria's boyfriend, Uncle Samuel was downstairs keeping him company.

Shereen lost herself in her thoughts, which wouldn't leave her alone lately. Memories of her and Mo bombarded her, taking her back to the happy times they spent together when they were children and these last six months since they started dating.

With Mo's wedding and Catarina's death, she'd been a little worried the time they'd spent apart might have changed them too much, and they might not like each other in the way they needed to make a marriage work. But every day they spent together, physically or video calling when she was in Leeds, fortified her belief that they were right for each other.

That fear which struck her the two times she'd received proposals before was definitely a thing of the past. When Mo proposed to her, she'd run to him heart and soul. The words had been dying to get out of her mouth even before he finished speaking. She'd known. Certainty had filled her every pore and, she'd known with him that she was home.

"Shereen, you do look beautiful," Auntie Gloria said from behind her, looking at Shereen in the reflection of the mirror. "This satin is beautiful. Stand up for me so I can have a proper look."

Shereen laughed. "Aunt Gloria, you've already seen me."

"Yes, but that was before we put on all the bells and whistles. That borrowed stocking is something else. Mo's mum has taste. From what your mum said, she's just as in love with you as your young man. Now stand up."

Not given a choice, Shereen stood up when Auntie Gloria placed her hand on Shereen's elbow and lifted. "Move her over to the middle of the room," Shereen's mum instructed.

Her mum and Auntie Gloria looked her up and down—from the veil at the top of her head to her mermaid, long-sleeved wedding dress which protected her against the slight chill in the May air and then her high heeled, bridal white platform shoes.

"You're like a fairy from another planet," Auntie Gloria said. "Isn't she, Rosa?"

Shereen's mum nodded, blinking continuously.

"Oh, don't start again, Rosa. Save it for the church; otherwise, you'll get me started. Shereen, let's go. It won't hurt to get to church a little early."

Shereen wanted to go too. The fear that something might happen and she wouldn't be able to marry Mo was turning her stomach into knots. She knew it didn't make sense, but she'd only feel better when she saw him.

Should I call him?

Shereen bit her lip. Was it okay for the bride to call the groom while getting ready? Would she look clingy? But then she shook her head.

He's my best friend.

She grabbed her phone on the dresser. "I'm going to the bathroom," she said.

She dialled Mo's number and put the phone to her ear with her right hand while her left hand tapped on the marble beside the sink.

"Hi, honey. You okay?"

Shereen sighed. She pushed the lid down on the toilet and sat down. "Yeah. I just wanted to hear your voice."

"I'm at the church. But I'm getting funny looks

from the boys. They said I'm crazy, that it was too early to come."

Shereen laughed. It was a little too early to be at the church already. "Why did you go so early?"

"I want to marry you as soon as possible. So if I'm early, and you don't make me wait because of that silly bride must be late belief, we can get married a little early."

Shereen laughed again, but warmth spread all over her insides. The fear unclawed itself and burst into nothingness. Mo was her best friend, who knew how to make her smile. Who knew when she was sad. And right now, he was committed to her. There was nothing to be afraid of.

She hung up soon after and went back into her mum's room. "Aunt Gloria is right. Let's go," she said. Her mum and Auntie Gloria were sitting down on the small sofa in the corner of the room and looked up at her. "I'm ready, and so is Mo. He's already at the church."

Auntie Gloria burst out laughing. "Goodness gracious me, what an eager pair. I know your mum wants grandchildren, but you don't have to rush like this." She stood up anyway.

Her mum gazed back at Shereen, an unreadable expression in her eyes. "If Mo's there, let's go then. He probably rushed everyone like you did. Let's not make you two love birds wait any longer."

The doorbell rang. Her mum lifted Shereen's train and walked slowly behind Shereen, and Gloria followed.

"Your friends are here," her mum said.

Shereen smiled, hearing the excited chatter from downstairs.

"I'm so sorry we are late. It's all my fault," Sophie said from the bottom of the stairs, wiping away a tear. "Gosh, Shereen, you look beautiful!"

Sophie wrapped Shereen up in a hug and kissed her cheek lightly. "Now I'm going to ruin your make-up." She pulled herself away and walked towards the sitting room.

"Stop there, Sophie!" Shereen called, from over Andrea's shoulder, who'd hugged her as soon as Sophie moved away. "It's okay. Accidents happen. And don't tell me you were just fussing and should have known better. You thought Ivy was seriously ill and took her to A&E. I'm sure that's what most mums would do. You didn't know it was indigestion, let alone that a couple of spoonfuls of medicine would make him better. It's my wedding day, and I command you to let go of any guilt and just be happy for me."

Sophie nodded.

"See, didn't I tell you Shereen would be cool about it. Seriously, you're just as excited as the bride, the way you are so nervous," Kate said.

Everyone laughed. Shereen loved Sophie, she was the most empathetic out of all her friends, but when she got nervous, she took forever to calm down. And usually, that happened after she'd been sick.

Kate and Heena hugged her too. "Now, let's check if Shereen survived all our hugs," Sophie said, eyeing her friend.

Shereen felt like a bug under a microscope. "I look fine, all of you. Seriously. This make-up is waterproof and everything. I was told it would stand the test of a million hugs and kisses. So chill." She moved to the kitchen and grabbed a glass.

"Sit down. Do you want water? I'll get it for you," Heena said, sliding the glass out of Shereen's hand.

Shaking her head, Shereen sat at the massive table. "How is Ivy?" She asked Sophie.

"Sleeping. Derek is with her. They won't make it to the church, but after resting, they'll come to the party."

Shereen nodded, glad. Auntie Gloria came in, and Shereen introduced her friends to her. She'd just finished when the bell rang again.

Excitement burst through Shereen. It must be Ben and the other Rodrigo children. Now everyone was here, and they could leave.

"Hi Mum!" Ben rushed into the kitchen. Shereen just about managed to catch him. "Today you're marrying Dad. I can call you Mum."

Those pesky tears filled Shereen's eyes again. Surely she'd cried way too much for the mascara to be able to handle it. She picked Ben up and sat down with him on her lap. "Yes." Was it possible to be too happy? Shereen felt like she was going to burst with happiness. Finally, her two dreams were coming true. To marry Mo and have children with him. With that one word, Ben had made this day complete.

Ben patted her chest. "I waited so long, Mum. Now I can call you Mum every day."

"Yes, Ben, you can." She looked at him. "You look as handsome as your father in that suit."

"Do I?" Ben asked all huge eyes and dimples.

Shereen smoothed her hand over the soft fabric of the tuxedo he was wearing. It fit his tiny shoulders to perfection but gave him a more serious look. She looked at the twins, one in a tuxedo just like Ben and the little girl in a white chiffon dress that reached her ankles. It matched Chantel's dress exactly, and even though the older girl – Maria's daughter - was fourteen now, she looked cute in it.

Dad walked in. "Let's take a picture before we go. First Shereen and the children, then Shereen with the bridesmaids, before we all take a selfie.

"Don't forget one of the bride and her parents," Kate called out.

"And me and Uncle Samuel," Auntie Gloria added. "I want one too."

Amongst the laughter, they took all the photos and squeezed into the massive limousine when it arrived outside. Mum and Dad followed behind with the Auntie Gloria and Uncle Samuel.

This was exactly what she pictured when she imagined her wedding, Shereen thought. All of her friends and family beside her to celebrate the day together. She looked at each one of the people in the limousine and smiled, hoping Mo wouldn't tire of waiting. They were going to be a little late after all.

***

"They are here," Tae Joon said beside Mo, at the entrance of the church where they were greeting guests.

Noah clapped Mo on the back. "Let's go inside, so you don't see the bride."

Bradley and Eli laughed, but they led the way inside the church. Mo walked up the aisle, feeling every thud of his shoes on the red carpet. To say he was nervous was an understatement. He'd woken early, unable to sleep, glad Ben was at his mum's. He'd felt compelled to visit Catarina. As he stood in front of her grave, it wasn't an apology he'd given her, for only visiting her once a week and starting a new life but words of thanks. He realised as he let the words out that he was thankful for their time together and for Ben.

"We'll give Ben the kind of life you've always wanted for him," he'd told her. Then he'd turned around and left, knowing that today was going to be his and Shereen's day.

He stood at the front of the church with Tae Joon, his best man, and looked at his family and friends, many of whom had been at his first wedding. He was much more nervous than he had been at his first wedding, and he knew why. Breathing in and out, he tried to calm himself down.

He knew how life could change in a heartbeat, how all your dreams could be snatched from you when you least expected it. He was afraid, he admitted to himself. But he didn't want Shereen to see he was nervous. She'd been waiting for this day a long time, and it was going to be perfect. He would use that fear to appreciate every day with her as a reminder not to take their life for granted.

Pushing his shoulders back, he stood tall. His eyes landed on Tae Joon's.

"You've got this man. And you are lucky I didn't make a move on Shereen, otherwise, she'd be mine."

Mo smiled. "Shereen is clever, and she knows who's going to treat her right. With me, she's going to be the only woman in this world in my heart."

"You got me there." Tae Joon smiled.

A movement to his left caught Mo's attention. His parents approached him. Mo looked at them, glad he'd been able to make them give up worrying about him spending the rest of his life alone.

Mum smoothed the lapel of his blazer. "It's going to be alright," she said, tears misting her brown-black eyes.

Dad nodded, eyeing Mo up and down. He patted Mo on the shoulder then pulled his mum back. "Look, Rosa is coming in. That means the bride will be in soon. So let's greet the in-laws and sit down. Tae Joon, take good care of our boy."

"Yes, sir," Tae Joon said.

Mo watched his parents greet Shereen's mum then sit down. Auntie Rosa blew him a kiss before sitting down too on the opposite side to his mum and dad.

"It's showtime," Brad said as the music played.

Mo faced the central entrance to the church, heart beating like a drum on steroids. As soon as Shereen appeared on her dad's arm, his heart stilled. Calm filled him. When Shereen's gaze arrowed on his face, he felt his lips tug up. He could swear her lips mirrored his. He watched as she walked up to him, one step at a time.

When she reached him, Uncle Andy placed her

hand on his. "Take care of my baby," he said.

Chest tight, Mo looked at the man who'd always treated him like a son. "I will," he said. He accepted Shereen's hand, and together they faced the priest.

"Dearly beloved, we are here today to celebrate the wedding of Shereen Beckley and Moises Benjamin Rodrigo…"

Mo listened to the priest's words, taking them in, resisting the temptation to look at Shereen and hold her hand.

"Now, the bride and groom will say a personal vow to each other before we proceed with the exchanging of rings," the priest said.

Mo looked at Shereen. He'd wanted to do this. He knew he didn't have to, and it had taken some convincing from his mum before the priest accepted. But he'd wanted to make a vow to her in front of all his family and friends during this marriage ceremony.

"Thank you for waiting for me. I will cherish every day of my life with you as if it was our last day. I promise to love you and take care of you every day of my life and be courageous enough to give you the things you most desire. I promise to be your best friend through the hard and the good times of our marriage."

He swallowed the lump in his throat. Seeing

Shereen tear up was doing strange things to him. He wanted to crush her to him then and hold her tight.

Shereen blinked. “I promise to love Ben as my first child and to be your best friend too, in the hard and good times.”

As they looked at each other, everything in Mo arrowed into Shereen’s eyes. The people and sounds around him disappeared. It was just the two of them at that moment. A throat cleared, and Mo blinked. He looked at the priest.

“Let’s exchange the rings.”

Ben and Jay moved forward, each carrying a ring on a satin, white pillow. Mo took Shereen’s ring from his nephew and took Shereen’s left hand.

“With this ring, I thee wed…” he vowed as he pushed the ring slowly on her ring finger.

Then he watched as Shereen smiled at Ben and took Mo’s ring from him.

“With this ring, I thee wed…” She said as she also slowly pushed the rings up Mo’s finger.

“You may kiss the bride,” the priest said.

Mo turned to Shereen and gazed at her. Finally, his wife.

Mine.

He reached his hands out to her cheeks and stared into her eyes. Anticipation burned there.

Hypnotised, he lowered his head until their lips touched. Tendrils of fire raced up his spine and spiralled out of control when Shereen opened her mouth to give him entry and wrapped her arms around him. He found her tongue and stroked it with his, feeling the fire intensify.

Whistles and catcalls for more penetrated his brain and he pulled back. Heat suffused his neck and face as he watched red fill Shereen's cheeks. Feeling like a teenager, he smiled and watched as her lips lifted too.

The priest cleared his throat. Twice. Mo turned to him.

"Sorry," he said, not at all apologetic but respecting the elderly priest's conservative nature. He didn't always have the same views as Father Thomas, but he respected how the priest stuck to his principles and admired his discipline and the way he cared for his parish.

Father Thomas cleared his throat again until the guests were silent. Then he ended the marriage ceremony. Mo took Shereen's hands and turned to face the entrance. He waited until the bridesmaids, ring bearers, and flower girls lined up in front of him, and Shereen then followed them to loud cheers.

***

Shereen held on tight to Mo's hand. He had her, and she had him. When she walked up the aisle, she was too nervous to look at the church or the family and friends sitting in the pews. Looking at Mo quieted the large butterflies flying in her tummy so she'd held onto his gaze. But now, she looked around. At the friends and family, at the beautiful flowers and organza decorating each pew. The church looked beautiful, completely different to when she'd visited with Mo to talk to the priest.

"Congratulations, Shereen and Mo."

Shereen waved at one of her mum's colleagues she'd known since she was a child. As they moved down the aisle, there were many more people to wave and smile at. From her side, her school friends had attended, and so had her editor and agent. As well as a few writing friends she'd made over the years. Her dad's family was small, and he was an only child, so not many people attended from his side. And although her mum's family was large, only two of her sisters attended. And she'd been grateful for that.

It felt like the whole Angolan diaspora in the United Kingdom was at their wedding. The groom's side was overflowing, and a lot of the Rodrigo family's friends were sitting on her side of the church.

Outside, Shereen's eyes closed against the stray confetti hitting her face. She giggled and looked at Mo, chuckling beside her and trying to avoid the barrage of confetti.

"Pictures," someone called.

They moved to the church greenery and squeezed together to take one picture of everyone present. It took forever to make sure everyone was in the picture, and they'd all be seen. Ben and the children stood in front of them, with her mum and dad and Mo's parents beside them.

They went to Regent's Park to take more pictures. It was one of her and Mo's favourite parks, even though they both found it too busy to have a quiet time for long.

"Now carry the bride, Mo. Let's see if you have the strength to carry your woman," Brad called out.

Shereen shook her head, laughing. The photo requests from Mo's friends and his brothers were starting to get ridiculous. She'd posed in so many different positions, she was starting to ache. They endured a few more.

"I can't do it anymore," she told Mo after a particularly ribald request, glad her parents and Mo's had already left for the reception venue.

"That's it, let's go to the saloon. I bet everyone is hungry," Mo shouted so everyone would hear him.

The limousine ride was just as lively. Luckily, the children's presence meant coarse comments were not allowed. Instead, Sophie, Heena, Kate and

Andrea felt free to tell Mo and the children all the hilarious anecdotes of her student life. After twenty minutes of that, Shereen attacked with stories about Mo's childhood.

At the reception venue, her friends and Chantel helped her get out of the car. Then, they waited until Noah, Brad, Tae Joon, Eli and Eli's friend Lucas joined them.

"They worked so hard to do this," Shereen whispered to Mo, awed by how well their friends and family had organised everything as they moved along, like a group that had been dancing together for years, everyone perfectly positioned. Libby was at the front, making sure the children knew where to go. Finally, they entered the saloon to loud cheers and clapping.

"The bride and groom will have their first dance, surrounded by the bridesmaids and men of honour," Mo's DJ cousin who'd travelled from Angola announced.

Libby took the children to one side of the room. The bridesmaids and groom's men kneeled in a wide circle in the middle of the dance floor. Shereen and Mo entered the circle to the first strokes of Roberto Carlo's amor infinito.

Mo held out his hands. Shereen placed hers in his, and followed him, swaying to the beat of the song. She was comfortable in his arms. She learned to waltz at a young age, when Zacchaeus taught the boys. Dancing and music was a huge part of the Rodrigo household; she was glad she'd learned to love all different types of dance and music there.

"I love you," Mo whispered in her ear.

"Love you back," she whispered too.

"Here they come, remember I told you about this," Mo said.

The song was nearly over, Rebecca and Zacchaeus came towards them. Shereen placed her hands in Zacchaeus' and watched as Rebecca led Mo towards her mum. Then Rebecca went to her dad. Shereen had warned her mum and dad about this, and she was glad when they took it in their stride. After dancing for a while, Uncle Zacchaeus nodded to her. He stopped by her dad and tapped on his shoulder.

Shereen danced with her father, reminded of the odd occasion he'd pick her up and dance with her.

"You've grown. I'm not sure I can pick you up anymore."

Was her dad thinking of the same memories? Shereen pecked him on the cheek. "You can tell me to grow up when I'm being silly, and you worry about me, and that's just as good."

"No regrets?"

Shereen cocked her head and looked at her dad. She knew she'd worried him and her mum by the way she'd refused two marriage proposals, and lived so far away from home and everyone she'd loved. Because she was about to turn thirty-three, he and her mum had begun worrying about grandchildren too. But all that mattered to him was her happiness. Even if he didn't get any grandchildren, if she were happy, he'd be okay.

"None at all. This is still my dream, Dad. I'm happy."

Dad nodded.

Another song started, and she danced with Mo again, a lump in her throat as the thought that her parents were dancing together at her wedding registered in her mind.

"It's now the time to cut the cake. Esteemed guests, let's celebrate this happy time with the couple," the DJ announced.

They danced and had fun, enjoying spending time with family and friends.

***

Shereen and Mo chose to start their honeymoon straight away. "We'll sleep on the plane," Shereen had answered when Mo asked if she wanted to spend the night at a hotel in London. They travelled to Barbados, staying in a cottage rather than in a hotel room so that they could have more privacy.

After dinner at the hotel restaurant, they

strolled through the beach. They took their shoes off and strolled, letting their feet dig into the sand as they walked. Waves lapped the soles of their feet as they smelled the salt in the air.

Shereen paused and turned to look far out to sea. She looked as far as her eyes could see, fascinated by the moon and the ribbon of light it left on the rolling water. Occasionally other couples strolled past, but for most of the time, they were alone.

"It's weird, isn't it? It's like we're the only people on the planet."

"Mmm." Mo let go of her hand and moved behind her. Sighing, he wrapped his arms around her and nibbled at her neck.

Shereen turned her head a little, loving the feel of his teeth and lips as he leisurely kissed and nipped. She covered his hands and closed her eyes. The gentle sound of the waves hitting shore reached her ears. A gull cried. Shereen's eyes opened and traced the bird's path as it flew over the sea. Lights shone in the distance, and sounds of lively music reached them.

"Do you want to go and see what's happening over there?" Mo had lifted his head and was looking towards the sound too.

"Not today," Shereen said. She grabbed Mo's hand. "Let's go back to our cabin."

Mo and Shereen entered their cottage, hand in hand.

"Do you want to have a glass of wine?" Mo asked.

Shereen shook her head. Butterflies danced freely inside her, somersaulting in her stomach, but she was ready for her wedding night. And so was he if the looks he'd been giving her were anything to go by.

When Mo picked her up, Shereen shrieked. She hadn't been expecting that at all. She snaked her arms around his neck and held on. He sat with her on his lap.

"Mrs Rodrigo, I want to make love to you."

Shereen chuckled. Talk about a way to remove the nerves. She palmed his cheek and kissed him quickly on the lips. "So do I," she replied. Then she kissed him again, but this time, Mo didn't allow her to escape.

"No more teasing," he whispered.

The End

To Download a Bonus Epilogue and subscribe to my Email Reader Group visit https://bookhip.com/WCAZTQP

I hope you enjoyed reading See Beneath Your

Perfect. If you did please help others discover the story by taking a short moment to leave a rating/ review at https://www.books2read.com/sb2.

Don't forget to check out See Beneath Your Beautiful, book 1 in the See Beneath Series and Smile Again, my contemporary short story collection.

Acknowledgement

To Trish, who joined me on the See Beneath Your Perfect Journey and lasted long enough to do the final edits for this beautiful piece of fiction. You helped make See Beneath Your Perfect the book it is today.

To my beta readers and cover designer, a massive thank you. You know who you are.

To my family and friends. Thank you for continuing to support me, even though you find it hard at times.

To my girls. My beautiful, wonderful girls. Thank you for bringing joy into my life. You make me so proud.

And to my husband. Thank you for being in my life.

About The Author

Eunice Nascimento

Eunice Nascimento strives to write stories that explore how people's life experiences affect their relationships. She's inspired by life, news, the people around her and enjoys writing tangled situations where true love wins out. By taking readers on an emotional roller-coaster, she hopes that they will find a delightful escape from the everyday in her books.

Eunice currently resides in London with her spouse and two children. When she's not writing or spending quality time with her family, she enjoys reading romance novels, watching K dramas, dancing salsa, bachata, and kizomba. Though she admits that lately she's more likely to watch YouTube dancing videos than to actually dance herself.

Visit Eunice at www.eunicenascimento.com, www.facebook.com/eunicenascimentowrites, www.instagram.com/eunicenascimento2015 and www.twitter.com/eunicemussage to learn more about her. Make sure to join her monthly newsletters for exclusive short stories about characters in the See Beneath World. Your can also follow her on goodreads at https://www.goodreads.com/author/show/17716240.Eunice_Nascimento.

Books In This Series

See Beneath

See Beneath is a Sweet Contemporary Romance Series about the children of the Rodrigo Family and their friends.

See Beneath Your Beautiful

Libby made herself a promise…
Noah's going to make her break it.

Libby's a strong, independent woman who made a pact with herself; focus on work, self-discipline, and above all else, no relationships. Driven by a traumatic past, she's held firm to this pact for her adult years… Until Noah threatens everything.

Noah's life is in order, he's lined up to meet a nice young woman. But when Libby stumbles into his life, everything derails and he wants to get to know her better. Something about her draws him in and he suspects she feels the same way. Noah is used to trusting his instincts and fighting for what he wants—and he has the perfect plan for sweet-talking Libby into his life.

Overcoming their differences in culture and upbringing won't be easy. Libby is unlike any woman Noah has dated. And Libby's certain his family doesn't approve of her. Can she overcome the ghosts of her past and find the courage to open her heart? Or will Noah learn that the business of love is beyond anyone's control?

See Beneath Your Beautiful is a heart-warming series standalone closed-door romance full of sizzling chemistry and a swoon-worthy property developer.

See Beneath Your Perfect

Shereen and Mo have been friends since they were three.
Shereen's loved him almost as long.
He married someone else—but fate is about to throw them together…

When a tragic loss leaves Mo widowed and a single dad, his best friend Shereen steps into his life to help. But when his son tells him that Shereen's his Earth mum while his departed mother is his heaven mum, Mo realizes that maybe it's time to move on. Of course, falling in love after loss isn't easy. Mo needs to work past his fear, his sadness, and his still-strong tie to his late wife.

Shereen's never admitted she's in love with Mo, and now she's not sure she ever can. Before, preserving their friendship meant more to her, and she watched him marry someone else. Losing him hurt her deeply, and no man earned her heart after him. So when the opportunity to try to make him hers arises, she leaps at the chance. But he remains steadfast and committed to his late wife. Maybe fate's keeping his love off-limits... or maybe she needs to discover how to make him understand she's loved him forever.

See Beneath Your Perfect is a series standalone closed-door romance with a sexy doctor and cute little boy wishing for a mum to cuddle up to.

Books By This Author

Smile Again

Smile Again Smile Again is a collection of 12 heart-warming stories of romance, family and friendship, guaranteed to make you smile no matter your mood. In Memories of Kessingland Beach, Sarah finally finds the courage to forgive herself and make peace with her Dad while in The Way to Mia's Heart, it takes a nudge from a friend to make Mia realise the chef at her favourite restaurant might be her Mr Right. Granny Square Afghans brings a new friendship which leads Debbie to confront her fear of water and in Janet's Dilemma, will Janet find the resolve to tell her husband what's bothering her?

Put your feet up and enjoy these as well as 8 other feel good stories in Smile Again.

A Note From Eunice

Thank you for reading See Beneath Your Perfect and embarking on the See Beneath World journey with me.

I loved writing Shereen and Mo's story. Mo has a special place in my heart because he is a haematologist who cares so much about the young people he looks after. Just like an unstoppable female consultant who did so much for my daughter and other children with sickle cell where I live. As for Shereen, well, there's a little bit of her in everyone of us isn't there?

If you read See Beneath Your Beautiful – Libby and Noah's story, you met Chelsea, Libby's bubbly best friend. Currently I'm working on Chelsea and Bradley's story as well as thinking about Tae Joon's life and his love interest. I'm actually torn about which story to publish first as I'm in love with both.

I hope you stick around for all the six books in the series, including Eli and his best friend Lucas'

novels.
Happy reading

Printed in Great Britain
by Amazon

81714888R00171